Also by Sophie McKenzie

GIRL, MISSING

SISTER, MISSING

BLOOD TIES

BLOOD RANSOM

SIX STEPS TO A GIRL

THREE'S A CROWD

THE ONE AND ONLY

THE MEDUSA PROJECT 1: *THE SET-UP*

THE MEDUSA PROJECT 2: *THE HOSTAGE*

THE MEDUSA PROJECT WORLD BOOK DAY SPECIAL:
THE THIEF

THE MEDUSA PROJECT 3: *THE RESCUE*

THE MEDUSA PROJECT 4: *HUNTED*

THE MEDUSA PROJECT 5: *DOUBLE-CROSS*

THE MEDUSA PROJECT 6: *HIT SQUAD*

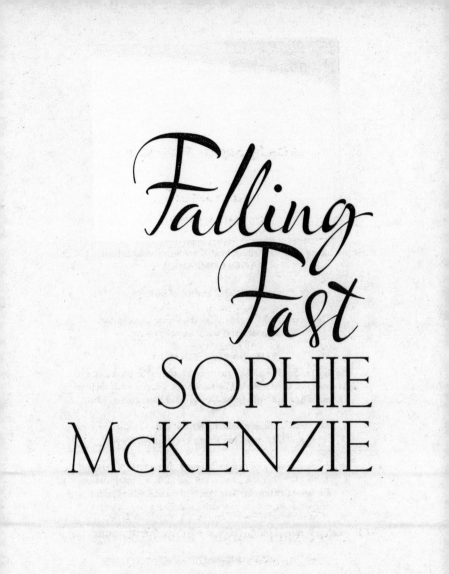

Falling Fast

SOPHIE McKENZIE

SIMON AND SCHUSTER

First published in Great Britain in 2012 by Simon and Schuster UK Ltd,
A CBS COMPANY.

Copyright © 2012 Sophie McKenzie

Simon & Schuster UK Ltd
1st Floor, 222 Gray's Inn Road, London WC1X 8HB

This book is a work of fiction. Names, characters, places and
incidents are either the product of the author's imagination
or are used fictitiously. Any resemblance to actual people
living or dead, events or locales is entirely coincidental.

A CIP catalogue record for this book is available from the British Library.

ISBN: 978-0-85707-099-9

1 3 5 7 9 10 8 6 4 2

Printed and bound by CPI Group (UK) Ltd, Croydon CR0 4YY

www.simonandschuster.co.uk
www.sophiemckenziebooks.com

To Eoin, who knows.

1

I stared out of the minibus window. It was raining and the pavements were a glistening grey. The houses and sky above were a softer, paler grey.

Grey. Dull. Boring. Like me. Like my life.

Maybe today would change everything.

Maybe.

Emmi peered past me. 'I think we're nearly there,' she said. 'So, River . . . you decided yet if you're gonna try for it?'

I swallowed. 'It' meant Juliet in *Romeo and Juliet*. We were on our way to auditions at St Cletus's – a local boys' secondary school that had invited Year 10s and 11s from our girls' school to try out for the female parts in the play.

Juliet was the main girl's part, of course. But that wasn't why I wanted it.

I looked out of the window again. The rain was falling harder now. I could hear it drumming on the

1

minibus roof even over the excitable chatter inside. There were about fifteen of us, mostly girls doing drama GCSE with Ms Yates or in her after-school drama group. For everyone else, I was sure, the auditions were just a laugh.

But not to me. I wanted to be Juliet in the play, because I wanted to be Juliet in real life.

I wanted to be in love. To be loved.

I was just sixteen and I'd never met a boy I really liked. I mean, I'd met a few I quite fancied and more than a few who were fun to chat to. But I'd never felt what you could possibly describe as love. I spent a lot of time imagining it, though. Imagining what he would look like. Tall and square-jawed, I thought. With deep, soft brown eyes that would melt me with their gaze, and dark, wavy hair curling onto his neck. He wouldn't be able to take his eyes off me. We'd move towards each other like magnets. Then we would talk and talk, discovering all the things we had in common, sharing our hopes and fears and dreams. And then, finally, we would kiss. A slow, deep, romantic . . .

'Hel-lo, River.' Emmi's amused voice broke through my thoughts. 'Are you going to audition for Juliet or not?'

I glanced at Emmi's heart-shaped, dimpled face. My best friend had a sharp prettiness – all sparkling dark eyes and dramatically-long, shiny hair. Unlike me, she was relaxed and confident. She was the obvious choice for Juliet.

But I knew she was the wrong one.

Whoever played Juliet had to at least be able to imagine what it would be like to really fall in love with someone else. I was pretty sure Emmi was no more able to do that than she was to stop flirting with every guy she met.

'Don't see why not,' I shrugged, trying to look unbothered about the whole audition process. 'I mean, if you're going for a speaking part, you might as well try for all of them. Not that I really care who I end up playing.'

Emmi grinned. 'Yeah, right, Riv.'

I shrugged again and went back to the window. My face burned. Trust Emmi to have seen right through me.

The minibus was pulling into a huge, mostly empty car park. Directly in front stood a large concrete school block. It looked deserted. I checked the time on my phone. Four p.m.

'Guess all the boys have gone home,' Emmi said. She sounded disappointed.

'Good.' I stood up and joined the queue to get off the minibus. 'The last thing we need is an audience.'

3

Emmi laughed. 'Isn't an audience exactly what we're here for?'

We got off the minibus and milled awkwardly in the car park. The rain had lightened to a soft drizzle. The absolute worst kind of weather for my hair, which gets all frizzy at the first sign of moisture.

A tall, very thin man with a high forehead and slicked back dark hair came striding towards us. A boy in the St Cletus school uniform of black trousers, white shirt and black-and-green striped tie trotted awkwardly beside him.

Ms Yates smiled nervously. 'That's Mr Nichols, the head of drama,' she said.

'Hello there,' the man boomed. For such a thin person, his voice was surprisingly deep. 'I'm Mr Nichols. Welcome to St Cletus's.' He beamed round at us all, casting a particularly warm smile at Ms Yates. 'Now let's get you in out of the rain.' He flung his arms out to indicate the boy beside him. 'If anyone needs the bathroom, James Molloy here will show you to the Ladies.'

Fifteen pairs of eyes swivelled to look at James Molloy.

He had sandy-coloured hair and a squishy, comfortable face. Underneath the flush of embarrassment creeping up his cheeks, I could see he looked nice. Nice, as in open and friendly.

4

You can't fall in love with nice.

Mr Nichols strode off towards the school building, indicating – with another exaggerated arm movement – that we should follow.

We all scuttled after him.

James Molloy had – surprise, surprise – gravitated almost immediately to Emmi's side.

'Hi,' he said hopefully, then blushed.

Emmi flashed him a big smile. 'Hi,' she purred. 'I'm Emmi.'

I giggled.

James Molloy gulped. He looked as if he was desperately trying to think of something to say.

We reached the large wooden door that Mr Nichols had just walked through. James held it open to let Emmi past, then dived after her, ahead of me.

'We're going to the sixth form common room,' he said. 'The auditions'll be in there.'

Emmi glanced over her shoulder and cocked an eyebrow at him. 'Will boys be watching?' she said in a silky voice.

She was really turning it on, but I could tell it was all for effect. Emmi liked to know that she could have any boy she wanted, but I'd never seen her bothered about any of them. Any other girl would have been labelled a slag, but Emmi somehow got away with it.

Poor James Molloy's face was now the colour of a tomato.

'Er . . . no,' he stammered. 'That is, not until the second round. Mr Nichols asked for people with main parts to stay after school to read with some of the girls when he's heard you all.'

'Ah . . .' Emmi said knowingly.

God, that meant having to do bits of the play with boys later. I glanced at Emmi. How come she wasn't in the slightest bit nervous about that?

'So the boys' parts are already cast?' Grace asked timidly.

Grace is my other really good friend. She's completely different from Emmi: shy and quiet . . . and she's been going out with the same guy for, like, forever.

James nodded, then led us along a series of chilly, rather rundown corridors, into a common room, complete with a pool table, a row of lockers and some bright red sofas.

'Please take off your coats and make yourselves comfortable.' Mr Nichols' booming voice resonated around its bare walls

'Sixth form common room,' James announced unnecessarily, staring at a patch of skin a few centimetres to the left of Emmi's nose.

Emmi nodded vaguely and wandered across the room. I turned to James.

'What part are you playing?' I said.

'Mercutio.' He blushed. 'Romeo's best friend. Which is cool, because the guy playing Romeo *is* my best friend.'

His eyes drifted sideways to where Emmi was self-consciously twisting her long hair in her hand. I watched his gaze flickering over Emmi's tall, slim body. She always seemed to manage to have her skirt a few centimetres higher than everyone else. She also wore her sweater tighter and her blouse unbuttoned further. When she walked she wiggled her bum and flashed off legs that went up to her armpits.

My heart sank. No way was I getting the part of Juliet instead of her. Not unless the guy playing Romeo was really short and Mr Nichols was practically blind.

I knew I should have been pleased for Emmi, but I wanted this so badly and I didn't stand a chance.

'Emmi's my best friend,' I said confidingly.

James Molloy looked down at me. For a second I saw myself through his eyes: I was short. I was dumpy. I was – *God*, I was like him. Squishy and comfortable.

At that point two other girls skittered over in fits of giggles and asked James to show them where the toilets were.

They all disappeared and I went to find Emmi and Grace.

'I'm so nervous,' Grace squeaked.

'For God's sake, Grace,' Emmi drawled. 'All you're doing is reciting a short poem. The worst that can happen is you'll end up a townsperson of Verona.'

Grace looked a little deflated. I don't think Emmi means it, but sometimes she can sound a bit harsh. After all, Grace was mostly here to support me and Emmi. Sure, she was doing drama GCSE, but performing wasn't really her thing.

I smiled at her. 'You'll be fine,' I said. 'You look really pretty.'

Grace smiled gratefully back at me. 'You look lovely too, Riv. I wish I had a figure like yours.' She sighed, then ran her fingers through her soft, strawberry blonde waves. 'And your hair really works the way you've got it tied back like that. You're so lucky it's so thick.'

Yeah, right. She was just being polite. Did I mention I have horrible frizzy hair and as for my body . . . well, maybe I'd look okay if I could lose half a stone . . . but however hard I tried, the weight never came off.

'Er . . . thanks, Grace.'

Emmi yawned. 'I don't know what you're getting anxious about,' she said to Grace. 'It'll be over soon, then you can phone Darren and tell him all about it.'

'Darren said he didn't like the idea of me being in a play at a boys' school,' Grace said.

Emmi rolled her eyes. 'Well, that's his problem, isn't it?'

I squeezed Grace's hand sympathetically, but the truth was I had no idea what Grace saw in Darren. He was geeky and spotty – while Grace was sweetly pretty, with her wide blue eyes and perfect skin. Plus, I was pretty sure he didn't have a passionate bone in his body. Mind you, looking at Grace's pale, anxious face, I wasn't sure she did either.

The thought depressed me. It seemed entirely possible Grace would go through her whole life never feeling an overwhelming, die-for-you love.

Lots of people probably didn't.

Not me, though. Please. Not me.

I closed my eyes and tried to remember the lines I'd picked for my audition.

The room fell silent. Mr Nichols cleared his throat.

'I think we'll start with a simple visualisation,' he said. 'Please, everyone, find a space to stand, then close your eyes and imagine a busy marketplace in old Verona. Observe the bustle, the townspeople

9

in their long gowns, all going about their business. Take time to smell the freshly baked bread, to squeeze the soft fruits on the stalls, to feel the warm sun on your back . . .' He droned on.

I sighed. This was exactly the sort of rubbish Ms Yates was into. I let my mind drift back to my ideal guy.

A minute or two later and Mr Nichols made us visualise walking into the centre of the marketplace and sitting in a circle on the ground.

'Now if you'd all open your eyes and find a seat . . . we'll start the auditions by going round the room,' he said.

There was a scramble for seats. I found myself perched on the arm of a sofa, next to Emmi.

'Okay, let's get going,' Mr Nichols said, suddenly brisk and businesslike. 'Please give your name before you begin.' He looked over to the door. 'James, tell the boys we'll be up in about half an hour. And shut the door on your way out.'

With a swift glance at Emmi's elegantly crossed legs, James backed out of the door. We all looked at Mr Nichols.

'A volunteer to start?' he said.

Everyone looked at their laps. Then I felt Emmi raise her hand beside me. 'I don't mind going first,' she said.

She sashayed over to the open space in the middle of the room. She faced Mr Nichols and smiled – a coy, shy smile. God, she hadn't even started and she was already acting.

Ms Yates nodded approvingly. She, like most of our teachers, loved Emmi because she was always prepared to speak out in class and because she was polite – at least to the teachers' faces.

She did a speech from the play – the beginning of the scene where Juliet is on her balcony and Romeo sneaks over to talk to her. She was good . . . She moved around naturally, and put loads of expression into her voice. But for all that, she never really sounded like she meant anything she was saying. I watched Mr Nichols. He was concentrating intently on her, his eyes following her as she moved. At the end she looked up at him from under her eyelashes. He nodded and smiled at Ms Yates.

Great.

After that we went clockwise round the room. Grace was next. Unlike Emmi she didn't move into the middle of the room. Instead, she stood where she was and recited her poem in a loud, clear voice.

She was actually quite good. A bit stiff maybe, but she put loads of expression into what she was saying and at least she remembered all the words. Asha Watkins forgot her poem, while Maisie Holtwood refused to even start. Two more girls just stood there, staring shyly at the carpet as they did a bit from the play.

On and on it went. After twenty minutes Mr Nichols was looking bored, his chin propped in his hands. A sly smile was sneaking across Emmi's lips. So far there was no one to touch her.

Thanks to the order we were sitting in, my audition was going to be last. I tried not to let the wait prey on my nerves.

A few more girls gave okay-ish performances. Daisy Walker, a tall girl with high cheekbones and intense dark eyes, was good. She moved about a bit, using her hands expressively like Emmi had done.

I felt more and more nervous. The time dragged and dragged. Then suddenly it speeded up and Mr Nichols' eyes were on mine – 'Yes?' he said.

2

I stood up. I was determined to take the stage like Emmi had done. That meant standing in the middle of the room.

It seemed a long way across the carpet.

As I faced Mr Nichols, I could feel my legs shaking. My heart pounded so loudly I was sure everyone would hear it.

'I'm River Armstrong,' I said nervously. 'I'm reading from Act 2, Scene 2.'

Too quick. Slow down.

I started, doing my best to keep my voice low and measured and my movements fluid.

I loved the lines I'd picked. When we'd studied *Romeo and Juliet* at school I'd been bored at first – all the fighting between their two families seemed stupid and pointless. And then I read the scenes between Romeo and Juliet. The love scenes.

I could feel my neck flushing with the intensity of

what I was saying. I looked up into the middle distance, seeing nothing and no one. And for a second I forgot I was dumpy River Armstrong, neither loved nor in love. And I became Juliet:

'My bounty is as boundless as the sea, my love as deep. The more I give to thee the more I have, for both are infinite.'

I could feel what that meant in my heart. In my soul.

I love you so much, so unselfishly, that it will never run out.

I clasped my hands together to try and stop them shaking. Then I slowly looked up from the carpet.

Mr Nichols was staring shrewdly at me.

And then he nodded. 'Good,' he said. He looked round the room. 'Now I'm going to leave you for just a minute to chase up some refreshments.'

He strode out.

Suddenly feeling massively self-conscious, I slunk over to Grace and Emmi.

'You were great, Riv,' Grace beamed up at me.

'Thanks,' I said, blushing.

Emmi raised her eyebrows. 'I thought you weren't that bothered which part you got?'

I could feel my whole face reddening.

Then Emmi grinned. 'Not that you fooled me.' She laughed. 'And you were good, you cow. I bet you get it.'

I smiled at her. 'I bet *you* do. You were brilliant.'

I squeezed her arm as I sank down onto the sofa.

Suddenly I was filled with relief that it was over. That I'd done it. And done it okay. At that moment I didn't care about love or playing Juliet. I was just glad to be with my friends.

'Hey, Grace,' I said. 'You were really good too. I think Darren might have to cope with you doing a play in a boys' school after all.'

Grace's pale face flushed with pleasure. 'Hey, Riv,' she breathed. 'D'you really think so?'

Mr Nichols reappeared after a few minutes with a tray of plastic cups, a plate of biscuits and a couple of cartons of juice.

As we each took a drink, he started speaking.

'The standard this evening has been very high.' He coughed. 'I will send the full list of girls invited to take non-speaking parts to your headmistress tomorrow, but for now I would like to see the following people for second readings so that I can assign the main parts: Daisy Walker, Grace Duckworth, Emmi Bains and River Armstrong.'

Yes. I was up for one of the female speaking parts. But which one would I get? There was Juliet, of course, plus her nurse – sort of like a nanny from when she was a child – and her and Romeo's mothers. At least I knew I had one of them.

One of them.

One of them wasn't enough. I didn't want to be a boring mother or a sensible nurse.

I *had* to be Juliet.

Everyone was chatting again. I glanced across at Emmi. Her lips were pressed firmly together. She wanted it too. I knew she did. More than she'd let on.

'Wow. I can't believe it,' Grace squealed, hurling herself at both of us. My plastic cup of orange juice tipped up against my jumper.

'Oh, no,' I said.

Grace leaped backwards. 'Oh, sorry, Riv. I'm really sorry.' She started dabbing at the dark grey stain on my jumper with her sleeve.

I wrenched it away. *God*. Now I was going to have to read with a big clumsy mess down my front.

'D'you want me to show you where the bathroom is?' James Molloy was back, smiling, his eyes flickering over to Emmi even as he spoke to me.

I nodded a grateful 'yes' and slunk off after him.

'I'll see you in a minute, River,' Grace called plaintively after us.

'Great. You can prepare something else to chuck at me when I get back,' I muttered under my breath.

James laughed. 'Don't worry,' he said pleasantly.

'No one'll notice.' He paused. 'Though I suppose you could take off your jumper. Er . . . I mean . . .' His face went red and he strode ahead a couple of paces.

I rolled my eyes at his white-shirted back.

It took several minutes to reach the girls' bathroom. James explained, blushing furiously, that there was only one in the whole school – as there weren't any girl pupils. Then I took a few more minutes to rinse off my jumper and check my make-up. I wasn't wearing much. Just a bit of mascara and lipgloss. I tried not to look too closely at my face – I didn't need my confidence knocked any further.

We hurried back to the common room. My hands were shaking again – I didn't want to be late on top of everything else.

Mr Nichols, Ms Yates and the girls from my school had been joined by four boys, all standing in a row against the wall beside Mr Nichols. My heart was pounding so hard it was practically bumping against my ribs. All the boys looked up as I walked in, but I kept my eyes on the floor, then glanced over at Emmi.

She smiled encouragingly. She looked irritatingly at ease.

Mr Nichols ran his hand through his slick dark

hair and started organising the readings. He got Grace to read Lady Capulet – Juliet's mother – with a boy with red hair, then asked her to try the Nurse, with me as Lady Capulet.

We didn't read much – just a few lines at a time. Mr Nichols kept switching the boys around and asking each of us to take different female parts – I completely lost track of who had read what. All I knew was we hadn't got to Romeo or Juliet yet.

Then, at last, Mr Nichols called over to a tall, dark-haired boy who'd been lolling against the wall at the end of the row.

'Flynn. Come and read with Emmi,' he barked.

The boy loped towards us. Though he didn't look up, there was something about him that commanded the room, that made you watch him.

He was Romeo. Had to be.

'Act 2, Scene 6,' Mr Nichols said with a flourish. 'Right, Flynn. Start with Romeo's line: *Ah Juliet, if the measure of thy joy . . .*'

Emmi wiped her palms on her skirt.

And Flynn, finally, looked up. He stared at the door as he spoke his first line, then he turned and looked at Emmi. His eyes wandered over her face as he spoke, then he looked away again.

I watched him, mesmerised. He was good. Unbelievably good. Way better than everybody else. His voice was strong and clear and flexible. The lines contained lots of weird, old-fashioned references that you'd have to really think about to understand. At least, that's what I'd had to do when I read them. But Flynn made their meaning clear just by speaking them.

As Emmi started with her lines, I stared intently at Flynn's face. He wasn't obviously good-looking. That is, he didn't have the melting brown eyes and square-jawed features of my fantasy guy.

But there was something about him. Something that meant you couldn't look away. The way his dark fringe flopped over his eyes. The way his nose turned up just the tiniest bit at the end. The way his mouth curved as he spoke. Above all, his face was so expressive. Just the blink of an eye or the curl of a lip and you could see his whole being flood with shock or anger. Or love.

I felt movement next to me and turned round. James Molloy was standing beside me, his eyes firmly fixed on Emmi's bum.

He must have sensed me looking at him, because he suddenly shifted his gaze to me – a sheepish, guilty look on his face.

'They're good, aren't they?' he whispered.

My mouth was dry. I nodded. 'What's his name?' I said. 'His first name.'

'Patrick,' James whispered. 'He hates it, though. You have to call him Flynn or he won't answer.'

I turned back to Flynn.

Emmi was still speaking.

Flynn was staring at her. He looked bored. Like he knew she didn't mean anything she was saying. Like he could see she wasn't feeling it.

Or maybe because he wished he was kissing her instead of having to listen to her speak.

Emmi finished.

'Lovely,' crooned Mr Nichols. 'Well done. Now, Flynn, the same again, but with River this time.'

I blushed at hearing my name said in front of all these boys . . . in front of Flynn. No one ever heard it right the first time. I was forever being asked to spell it and while I rarely got teased like I had at primary school any more, sometimes people made a face that suggested they thought it was weird . . . or funny . . .

I didn't want Flynn to laugh at me too.

Emmi stepped backwards and I took her place, my copy of the play trembling in my hands.

Flynn was an arm's length in front of me now. God, why was I so short? My eyes were level with his chest. I stared at it. His tie was loose, his white shirt untucked. As he read his lines, I could hear the same expressiveness I'd noticed before. But this time

I could tell he was only going through the motions. Like his mind was on something else.

Emmi, probably.

I looked up into his face just as he said his last line:

'Let rich music's tongue unfold the imagin'd happiness . . .'

Our eyes met. *Oh my God*. His gaze pierced right through me, like he was trying to see who I was. Who I *really* was.

No one had ever looked at me like that.

And his eyes were beautiful. Greeny-gold. Set the perfect distance from each other.

'. . . that both receive in either by this dear encounter.'

There was a pause. *Damn*. It was my turn. I had completely forgotten what the next line was. I bent over the play in my hand, searching desperately for it.

Flynn's finger landed on the page in exactly the right place.

I felt myself blush as I started reading.

I put all the feeling I had into what I was saying. At first I was too self-conscious to look up. When I finally did, Flynn was frowning slightly.

'. . . But my true love is grown to such excess . . .'

And then I realised why he must be looking puzzled.

My voice had shrunk to a whisper.

In the same instant I knew why. Juliet was basically saying this incredibly intimate, powerful thing about how her love for Romeo was so huge that she couldn't get her head round the half of it. And I was saying the lines as if it was just me and him in the room.

I immediately raised my voice. Way too loud.

'. . . *I cannot sum up half my sum of wealth.*'

Flynn jumped back, startled, presumably, at the sudden rise in volume.

Everyone else in the room laughed.

Oh God.

After that it was hopeless. We tried another scene. I stumbled over the lines, then remembered the stain on my jumper and tried to cover it with my copy of the play.

By the time I finished, Flynn was staring at me as if I was mad and titters of amusement were floating round the room.

Mr Nichols got Daisy Walker to read with Flynn, then we all trooped downstairs and back onto the minibus.

I pretended to be cheerful on the way back to school, but inside I was dying. Emmi kept saying that I'd done fine, but I knew she was just being kind.

I'd made a complete mess of that second reading.

Because of Flynn. Because of the way he'd looked at me with those intense green-gold eyes. Because he was a brilliant actor.

I struggled to put it out of my mind, joining in with Emmi when she teased Grace about Darren, then teasing Emmi myself about how much James Molloy had fancied her.

Neither of them teased me. Which meant, I knew, that I really, really had made a total idiot of myself.

My one comfort was that Emmi clearly thought I'd screwed up because I was nervous about getting the part, not for any other reason.

Two days later the four of us who'd been up for speaking parts got called into Ms Yates's room. She made a big show of saying how we were representing the school and how she expected us to maintain the highest standards of behaviour whenever we attended rehearsals.

Blah, blah, blah.

And then she gave out the parts.

Grace was Lady Capulet, Juliet's mother. Daisy was Lady Montague, Romeo's mother.

I held my breath.

And she said it.

Emmi was Juliet. I was the Nurse.
The Nurse. Short. Dumpy. Nice.
Nice.
My heart sank.
You can't fall in love with nice.

3

Rehearsals began the following Monday.

I got ready for school that morning very carefully, then examined myself in the long bathroom mirror.

My grey school sweater didn't cling snugly like Emmi's jumpers always managed to. It bulged out unattractively over my boobs, then settled into stiff, ugly folds just below my waist.

There was no getting away from it.

I looked fat. Bulky at the very least.

God, I really was the perfect choice to play Juliet's ex-nanny or Nurse or whatever she called herself.

I sighed and stroked mascara up my eyelashes.

I'd spent a lot of the weekend thinking about Flynn. Wondering about him. He intrigued me – the way he'd made everyone in the room aware of him just by walking across it, the weird contrast between how bored he'd looked most of the time and then the intense interest in his green-gold eyes when he'd looked at me, like he really wanted to know who I was.

That look, on its own, made him unlike any boy I'd ever met.

I was determined to talk to him later. To find out about him. He must be really into the play to speak his lines as well as he did. I could imagine him sitting in his bedroom, hunched up against his pillows, reading his way through Romeo and Juliet's love scenes. Just like I had done.

He probably read all sorts of books. Maybe even poetry. A shiver slithered down my spine. I knew it wasn't love I was feeling. I didn't even really fancy him. I was just . . . well . . . interested.

Then Emmi's pretty, flirtatious face flashed into my head.

Flynn wasn't going to notice me. He wasn't going to see past her – the fake Juliet in front of him.

I put down my mascara and leaned against the long mirror.

'OY. SWAMPY.' Stone – my younger brother – was yelling from outside the bathroom.

I sighed. Stone is nearly fourteen and the biggest jerk in the universe. He was full of himself for weeks after he started calling me Swampy. It's a mickey-take on my name being River, you see. And because

26

my hair is apparently the colour of mud and my eyes the colour of ditchwater.

'HOW MUCH LONGER YOU GONNA BE IN THERE?' Stone thumped the door.

I reluctantly peeled myself away from the bathroom mirror. No way was I letting Stone in until I'd finished – but if I didn't hurry up, he'd get Mum on my case. And I really didn't want a row this morning.

I picked up my mascara again and leaned towards the glass.

There was nothing good about my face. My nose was too blobby, my eyes set too close together, my mouth too small.

'SWAMPY. DID YOU HEAR ME?' Stone yelled again.

'Just a minute,' I shouted.

Stone swore loudly, then I heard him stomping off towards the stairs.

Up until six months ago, Stone'd been quite nice. This shy, sweet kid who got on with everyone and spent most of his time collecting football stickers. It felt like he changed overnight, though I suppose it couldn't really have happened that quickly. Now he seemed to hate everyone and everything and spent all his time locked in his bedroom listening to loud, aggressive rap.

Mum says he's a walking teenage cliché and that I should just ignore him.

I moved closer to the mirror and finished applying the mascara. Stone wasn't wrong about my hair and eyes. I had to admit it. Dull brown and dirty grey.

Mum was waiting for me just inside the front door. She was all dressed up for work in a blue suit, her hair carefully done in a consciously messy, flicked-back style. You'd never guess she used to wear long, hippy skirts and smoke joints with Dad after Stone and I had gone to bed.

'I haven't got long,' she said. 'I just wanted a quick word.'

I stared at her. Mum and I look alike. Even I can see it. We've got the same dark hair and grey eyes. The same heavy features. Only they suit Mum. Somehow she carries them off.

'River?' she said impatiently. 'This is important.'

'What is it?' My mind ran over the possibilities. Maybe Mum was secretly dying of some rare disease? No. She would hardly tell me about that just as she was leaving for work. Maybe it was Stone. Maybe he'd been nagging her about us swapping bedrooms again. Mine was twice as big as his. No way was he having it.

'I wanted to talk about tonight,' Mum said, checking her watch.

I frowned. Tonight? What was happening tonight? God, it wasn't her birthday again, was it? We'd forgotten it last year. She'd gone mental on us. But no, Mum's birthday was in February. And this was late September.

'It's the play you've got involved with,' she said. 'Where it is and everything.'

I shook my head. 'What . . .?'

Mum sighed. 'You know I've always treated you as an equal, River, so I'm not telling you what to do.' *Right.*

'I'm just saying it's in a boys' school. As in a Catholic boys' school where no girls are normally allowed. And you haven't . . . well, I'm just saying, as an older woman with a bit of experience, I know what boys are like. At that age they're mostly going to be interested in getting as far as they can and . . .'

'For God's sake, Mum,' I snapped, too shocked and embarrassed to sort out all the different things I was feeling. How dare she try and warn me off boys she didn't even know? I thought of Flynn and the way he had looked at me. Into me. That wasn't about sex and stuff.

'Look, I just wish my mother had talked like this to me.' Mum sighed, her cheeks reddening slightly. 'But the truth is they'll be after whatever they can get.'

I stared at her, feeling my own cheeks burn, as if Mum's blushes were now flowing into me.

'Yeah, Swampy.' Stone slouched up behind Mum, a sneer on his spotty face. 'And most of them won't be all that fussy about who they get it with.'

'Stone, be quiet.' Mum rolled her eyes, but I could see she wasn't actually disagreeing with him. In fact, that was her real point, wasn't it? That boys kept artificially away from girls most of the time were bound to be so desperate that they'd try and do it with anything that moved – even something as hideous as me.

Tears pricked at my eyes. I didn't want either Mum or Stone to see how upset I was.

'Right,' I snapped.

I stomped outside, slamming the front door shut behind me.

4

I got more and more nervous as the day went on. By the time Emmi, Grace, Daisy and I got on the bus to go to St Cletus's that afternoon, my stomach was twisted into a big knot.

'No school minibus today, then,' Emmi said bitterly. 'You'd think they'd send cars for us, seeing as we're helping them out by being in their stupid play.'

For some reason Emmi was pretending to find the whole thing a massive drag. She said she'd even considered turning down the part of Juliet. 'All those lines,' she'd groaned. 'And I didn't fancy *any* of the boys we saw the other day.'

My heart leaped at this. If Emmi didn't intend to get her claws into Flynn, I'd have more chance to talk to him. I was trying to think how to encourage her to pull out of the play altogether, when Grace peered round at us.

31

'There'll be other boys, Emmi,' she smiled. 'Loads in the rest of the cast, then all the ones who help backstage.'

Emmi's eyes brightened. 'True,' she said. 'And what with you being with Darren and that Daisy Walker . . .' she lowered her voice '. . . looking like she's totally up her own backside, there'll be loads to choose from for me and River.' She grinned. 'Hope we don't both go for the same guy, Riv.'

I gritted my teeth.

We'd been given permission to skip the last – free – period of school in order to get to St Cletus's by the end of their school day. The bell was ringing as we walked into the big, stone entry hall and found the bursar's office on the left. The secretary told us to wait outside while she buzzed the staffroom for Mr Nichols.

We lolled self-consciously against the office door as streams of boys of various ages and sizes stumbled past, wide-eyed and gawping. There was a lot of pushing and shoving and pointing, though none of them actually came over and talked to us.

'God, you'd think they'd never seen a girl before,' Emmi whispered to me.

I swallowed, remembering what Mum had said this morning. Still, none of these boys were Flynn.

After a few minutes the entry hall started to clear. James Molloy came bumbling over, a big grin on his slightly flushed face.

'Hi,' he said, to Emmi's left arm. 'I'm supposed to take you to the rehearsal room.'

I rolled my eyes at Grace. She smiled back. That was the good thing about the way me and Emmi and Grace were friends. Whenever something was happening to one of us, the other two were always there to share it.

My heart was pounding by the time we reached the rehearsal room. It was another classroom. Bigger than the one we'd used before, with all the desks pushed back against the walls. It was distinctly shabby too – with a few posters and bits of coursework pinned up on peeling wallpaper and a large, cracked whiteboard propped next to the door.

I looked swiftly round the room. My heart beat fast. I didn't want to admit it to myself, but I knew I was looking for Flynn.

There were at least ten boys lounging against the desks by the walls. Most of them were watching Emmi – who had dragged a blushing Grace into the middle of the room and was chatting to her ultra-casually, pouting her lips and raking back her hair as she talked.

I looked along the row of boys. Flynn wasn't here.

How could he not be here? He had the main part. I had a sudden and terrifying thought. Suppose something awful had happened to him and he'd pulled out of the play?

'You okay?' James Molloy had sidled up to me, unnoticed.

'Mmmn,' I said. 'Fine.'

'Er . . . your name's . . . er . . . River, isn't it?' James said.

I stared at him.

'Yes,' I said. 'Why?'

'Nothing,' James stammered. 'I just wondered. You said you were Emmi's best friend and . . . and I was thinking . . . I was just curious. Well, um, every-one is . . .'

He stuttered to a stop.

I frowned. 'Curious about what?' I said.

James gazed at Emmi. 'One of the other guys wanted to know . . . er . . . if she . . . if you know . . . there was . . . It's just, um, you're like her best friend. You said.'

I remembered something James had said the first time we'd met.

'You're Flynn's best friend, aren't you?' I said.

James shrugged. 'I guess.'

'Where is he?' I asked nonchalantly. 'Shouldn't he be here for the rehearsal?'

James nodded. 'He should be. But he told Mr Nichols he had a family emergency. Had to go home straight after school.'

'Oh.' I was bitterly disappointed. But at least Flynn was still doing the play. There would be other rehearsals, after all. I glanced sideways at James, hoping he hadn't noticed how deflated I'd sounded. He was still staring at Emmi.

'She doesn't have a boyfriend,' I said.

James looked round at me, startled.

I grinned. 'Well, that was what you wanted to know, wasn't it?'

The rehearsal lasted just over an hour. Mr Nichols got everyone to read through the first couple of acts. He said Romeo's lines himself. That must have been a bit weird for Emmi, but she kept her head down, concentrating hard on what she was reading, so I couldn't see her expression.

Afterwards some of the boys came over and tried to talk to us. I stood between Emmi and Grace, feeling ugly and awkward. Emmi was in her element, tossing back her hair and flashing dazzling smiles at them all. Grace looked nervous, but sweet. I could see several of the boys, clearly intimidated by Emmi's hard, sexy confidence, make a beeline for Grace. She giggled with them, looking up at them coyly from under her eyelashes.

I sighed. It was just a game to them. A dance. No one saying what they really felt. Everyone trying to be something they weren't. Putting on an act.

A few guys tried to speak to me, but I didn't really talk back. I didn't know how to join in and was torn between envy at the ease with which Emmi charmed everyone and irritation at the pointlessness of the whole thing. Soon, I slipped away and got the bus home by myself.

We went back on Thursday for another read-through – this time of the last three acts. Flynn still wasn't there. The same family emergency, James said mysteriously. But he didn't offer up the details and – because it was Flynn – I couldn't ask.

By the following Monday I had pretty much convinced myself he wasn't going to be there. Even if he was, I reckoned, I'd built him up in my mind and when I saw him again I was going to see he was really no different from the other boys.

It was a smaller rehearsal this time. Emmi and I went on our own. James came and took us up to the classroom we'd used on the first day, the one in the sixth form block. Three boys were already in there – the red-haired guy who I knew was playing Lord Capulet, Juliet's father, and two shorter guys who explained they were Servants 1 and 2.

James hung around for a while, chatting to Emmi's right shoulder, then bumbled off, mumbling something about not being in the scene we were rehearsing.

Act 1, Scene 5. The scene where Romeo and Juliet meet.

The door swung open. Mr Nichols came in. He was wearing a long scarf round his neck. It trailed down the side of his rather shapeless jumper. A stocky boy with a shock of blond hair strolled in beside him. I recognised him from the previous rehearsal. He was playing Tybalt, the guy Romeo kills.

Mr Nichols smiled distractedly at Emmi and me, then strode to the front of the room. He leaned against the teacher's desk and crossed his long, thin legs.

'I thought we would tackle a crucial scene tonight,' he said. 'The build-up to and first meeting of the Verona Two.'

The Verona Two was Mr Nichols' way of referring to Romeo and Juliet. He always chuckled when he said it. Nobody else ever did.

Mr Nichols absently wound his scarf a second time round his neck. 'Right,' he said, 'we'll start with . . .' He suddenly blinked rapidly. 'WHERE THE HELL IS FLYNN?'

He glared round the room.

All faces were blank. Then the door opened and Flynn strolled in.

5

'Sorry I'm late, sir,' Flynn said, not sounding sorry at all. He loped over to the nearest desk and leaned casually against it. 'Something I had to do after class.'

My heart pounded.

Flynn was extraordinary. Everyone was looking at him, and yet he didn't seem the slightest bit embarrassed.

'Right, well you're here now.' Mr Nichols coughed nervously.

I held my breath. Was that it?

Mr Nichols hesitated. I was sure he wanted to tell Flynn off properly, but something was holding him back.

Flynn stared at the teacher, his arms folded, a look of contempt on his face.

Mr Nichols turned his attention to the two boys playing Servants 1 and 2. They started saying their lines. Badly. Mr Nichols stopped them and explained in some detail what the lines meant. The boys gave lots of meaningful nods and 'oh yeahs', snatching looks at Emmi whenever they could.

I was avoiding looking at Flynn. The power of his presence was making me feel off balance somehow. I couldn't explain it. He was like a thunderstorm waiting to happen. Like when the air gets all heavy and you can almost feel the rumbling before you hear the thunder itself.

Very slowly, I raised my eyes a little, so I could see his face. He was staring at his shoes. They were worn and scuffed. In fact – I stared at his shirt and trousers – all his clothes looked worn. I hadn't noticed before, but the knees of his trousers were shiny, almost threadbare, and you could see lines at the bottoms of the legs where the hems must have been let down.

None of this stopped him from looking totally cool.

Suddenly the hairs on the back of my neck prickled. He was looking at me, I *knew* he was. Oh God, he'd seen me staring at him. I averted my eyes to the floor, then let them travel sideways.

I was still sure he was looking at me. I glanced up.

The intensity of his stare almost knocked me out. His face was rigid. Furious. Almost like he was challenging me not to laugh at him. I stared back; a fish caught on a hook. Why was he so angry?

My heart was pummelling at my chest now, so loudly it was drowning out Mr Nichols. I wanted to look away. But I couldn't. It was like Flynn was holding me in his gaze, pinning me down.

As we looked at each other, the hard look in his eyes softened. He wasn't smiling exactly, but at least he didn't seem angry any more.

I gazed at him, mesmerised by his face, by the shape of it, the lines of it. It wasn't an obviously good-looking face, maybe, but there was something about it – something . . . well . . . beautiful. His eyes were certainly beautiful. In the bright overhead light they shone gold, like a lion's.

And then Mr Nichols' voice boomed out more loudly. 'Once more, then, and we'll move on to Romeo noticing Juliet for the first time.'

Flynn looked away.

As everyone bustled about, saying lines, listening to explanations, Flynn moved slowly towards the centre of the room. He walked, as before, in that loping, slightly swaggering way of his. This hot, powerful glow radiated through my whole body. It was terrifying how strong it was. How it took me over. How I knew what it meant, instinctively, even though I'd never ever felt anything like it before.

41

I wanted him to touch me. To kiss me . . . I looked down at my hands. They were actually shaking.

Flynn started speaking. *Oh my God.* I'd forgotten what a brilliant actor he was. He was in a totally different league from the others. He finished his speech, his voice low and trembling.

'*Did my heart love till now? Forswear it, sight;*
For I never saw true beauty till this night.'

He walked back to where he'd been standing before, against the desk. I couldn't tear my eyes away from him. But he didn't look at me again.

The next part of the scene involved the boys playing Lord Capulet and Tybalt. I was oblivious to what they were doing. I was oblivious to everything except Flynn. And then I remembered Emmi. Had she noticed? I whipped round, expecting to see her watching me with raised eyebrows. *Phew*. She was poring over her script, frowning.

Sensing my gaze, she glanced up and grinned, beckoning me towards her.

'See any cute boys yet?' she whispered.

I grinned back and shook my head. What had just happened with Flynn was private. Personal. I didn't want to be teased about it – even by my best friend.

'Me neither. Though he's all right, if I had to.' She jerked her head towards the blond boy playing Tybalt. 'His name's Alex.'

I stared at him. Alex/Tybalt was thickset, with bland, regular features and a strong chin. Nice-looking, but nothing special.

Nothing special. Like me.

I suddenly remembered how ugly and dumpy I'd looked in the mirror this morning. I glanced at Flynn. He was frowning over his script. Like Emmi had been.

My heart sank. I had no hope. Who was I kidding?

'Right, everyone. Now before we begin the section of the scene where the Verona Two actually meet,' Mr Nichols boomed, 'who can tell me what the scene is *really* about?'

Deathly silence.

'What I mean is, who can tell me what actually *happens* in this scene.'

More silence. Then Alex tentatively raised his arm.

'Yes?'

'Er . . . Romeo kisses Juliet,' he said.

'Ye-es,' Mr Nichols said slowly. He wound the end of his scarf round his hand. 'But what happens before that?'

The silence filled the room.

Mr Nichols coughed. 'Okay, let's make it real, here. What has to happen before you kiss someone?'

Someone sniggered. No one attempted to answer.

'Come *on*.' Mr Nichols sounded irritated. 'Don't tell me you've never tried to kiss anyone before.'

More sniggering. My gaze flickered round the room. Everyone, including Emmi, looked totally embarrassed. Except for Flynn. Even in my one-second reconnoitre I could tell that he was more bored than embarrassed.

'Right.' Mr Nichols rolled his eyes and pointed at Alex. 'You. What has to happen before you kiss a girl?'

Alex looked appalled as he realised there was no way to escape answering the question. Long pause. 'Dunno, sir,' he finally stammered. 'Er . . . it just happens.'

'It "just happens",' Mr Nichols said sarcastically. 'I see, so you see a girl walking along the street and you go up to her and it "just happens" . . .'

A titter of nervous laughter drifted round the room. I think I may have joined in with it. Flynn didn't.

'Come on. What happens first? Matlock?'

Mr Nichols turned to Servant 1.

He shrugged. 'Dunno, sir. Touching?'

Mr Nichols sighed deeply. 'Dear God,' he said. 'Right. So you see a girl in the street. You go up to her. Grab her. And *then* you kiss her.' He shook his head. 'Tell me, Matlock, how's that approach working for you?'

A richer rumble of laughter echoed round the room.

'Come on, everyone,' Mr Nichols said brightly. 'It's not rocket science. What has to happen before you kiss someone?'

'You talk, sir.' It was Flynn. His voice steady, his eyes down.

'Yes.' Mr Nichols clapped his hands together. 'Yes, Flynn. You *talk*. That's what Romeo is doing here. He's chatting Juliet up. Now, how does he do it?'

'He tries to make her laugh, sir,' Flynn said, still with his head bowed.

'Exactly. Right, now let's have the lines. No actual kissing required, thank you.'

I could feel Emmi breathing a sigh of relief beside me.

She moved forward to where Flynn was standing. Mr Nichols directed them both into the middle of the empty space. They each said a few lines. Then Mr Nichols stopped them and made them explain them. Flynn seemed to have no problem with this. Emmi, on the other hand, grew red in the face as she struggled to make sense of what she'd been saying.

Mr Nichols frowned. 'Right, guys, okay, so Romeo is angling for a kiss while Juliet's quite happy to shake hands, as it were. They're talking about

45

pilgrims and saints and Juliet points out saints use their lips in prayer. Romeo as a "pilgrim" asks Juliet as a "saint" to grant his prayer for a kiss – "*let lips do what hands do*" – and Juliet says: "*Saints do not move, though grant for prayers' sake.*" Can anyone tell me what she means?'

I sat there, the blood pounding in my head. I knew what Juliet's line meant. I wanted Flynn to know I knew. And yet . . . and yet . . . it was terrifying to speak it out loud.

Mr Nichols' gaze drifted across the room. 'Anyone? Just jump in.'

I took a deep breath and blurted it out. 'I think Juliet is flirting . . . like, she's hinting she won't make the first move but she'll go there if *he* does . . . I mean, she'll grant him his prayer and kiss him . . .'

'*Yes.*' Mr Nichols punched the air.

Emmi nodded, clearly relieved.

'And *now* what does Romeo do?' Mr Nichols demanded.

'He kisses Juliet and says by granting his prayer she's taken his sin away,' Flynn said quietly.

'*Yes.* And then?'

Flynn caught my eye. I knew he knew what the next lines meant, but he was waiting for me to speak.

Letting me answer.

I turned to Mr Nichols. 'Juliet makes out that now,

46

cos of him kissing her, her lips are all covered with his sin,' I stammered, 'which is gross. But she only says it cos she wants him to kiss her again.'

'*Yes*.' Mr Nichols was on his feet. 'And then?'

'He kisses her again,' Flynn said. 'To get his sin back off her. So she doesn't have to carry it. It's clever cos he's making out he's doing her a favour. But really it's what he wants to do.'

As he said those last words, he glanced over at me again.

That hot, powerful feeling I'd had before flooded through me, stronger than ever.

Emmi stepped forward.

I watched her doing the scene with Flynn – speaking *our* lines. I was jealous. *Really* jealous. I couldn't help it. Then it was my turn to speak. As I said my lines to Romeo, I didn't look him in the face. I didn't dare.

After we'd gone through the whole scene, Mr Nichols took us all down to the sixth form common room where someone had laid out some more juice and biscuits. For some reason, Emmi was in a bad mood and had already told me twice that she wanted to go soon. We'd already planned to go back to Grace's for pizza so I was going to have to leave with the others.

But I didn't want to go. Not yet.

I darted over to Alex – Emmi had said he was all right, hadn't she? I murmured in his ear that she'd told me she'd like to talk to him.

It worked. Thirty seconds after I'd scurried away Alex wandered over and started in on some hard-core chatting up.

Emmi was already giggling as I headed for the orange juice. I just needed something to do with my hands before I turned round. Before . . .

I sensed him before I saw him. Felt the thunder-storm circling above my head.

'Are you Catholic?'

I looked round, my hand poised over a plastic cup.

Flynn was gazing down at me, his eyes so intense they almost peeled my skin away.

'Er . . . no,' I said.

Brilliant, River. Sparkling repartee.

'Oh.' Flynn sounded mildly surprised. 'I just thought . . . cos you seemed to understand all that stuff about the saints and sins so well . . .'

I could feel my mouth moving involuntarily. Why was he asking me about being Catholic? Then I remembered that this was a Catholic boys' school. Maybe he wasn't allowed to go out with anyone who wasn't the same religion as him.

I found some words. 'I'm sorry I'm not . . . Catholic, I mean.'

Damn. How stupid did that sound?

'Don't be sorry,' Flynn smiled. 'I think it's great you're not.'

I caught my breath. I'd never seen him smile before. It transformed his face, bringing it alive with charm and fun and a whole new level of sexiness.

Then he turned and walked away. A minute later Emmi was hissing in my ear about how boring Alex was – though she'd get with him if she had to.

We left.

I looked at Flynn before we walked out of the common room. But he didn't see me.

He was talking to the two Servants and Lord Capulet, holding them spellbound.

6

'How's the play going?' Mum's voice was all fake cheery. The tone she uses when her mind's really on something else. When what she's really saying is: *my time is precious, but I've set aside five minutes for a Proper Chat.*

I looked up from the kitchen table where I was bent over my script. 'Play's going fine,' I said.

It was Saturday morning, two weeks after that first real rehearsal. Flynn hadn't been at the next one and I wasn't needed for the one after that, so I hadn't seen him since he'd done that weird thing of asking me if I was Catholic.

Mum peered over my shoulder.

'You still learning your lines?' she said. 'I'd've thought you knew the whole play off by heart by now.'

I closed the play so that she wouldn't see I was actually reading – rereading – the scene where Romeo declares his love to Juliet. A scene in which, unsurprisingly, Juliet's nurse did not feature.

Mum slid into the chair beside me. She laid a hand over the play, and my fingers which rested on top of it.

'Is everything all right, River?' she said. 'It's just you've been very quiet since you started these rehearsals.'

I shrugged, staring down at Mum's fingernails. They were painted with a dark blue base, and decorated with silver stars and tiny crescent moons. Mum's nails are the only remotely alternative thing about her now. Her leaving all that hippy stuff behind was what made my parents split up. It happened a few years ago, half-way through my Year Seven. Mum told me recently she'd felt that she'd grown up and Dad hadn't. I'm not sure it was that straightforward. I think, maybe, that she just got tired of pretending to be someone she wasn't.

She works in an office now – still spouts all this stuff about capitalist oppressors and management bastards, but you can tell it's only skin deep. Come the war to end corporate global tyranny and Mum'd be first out the back door – looking for somewhere to do her nails in peace, probably.

'You know you can tell me anything,' Mum said softly. 'Whatever it is, I promise you I've been there already.'

I looked up at her. No way had she ever let herself

51

feel like Flynn made me feel. Even when she was pretending to live the hippy life, she was always far too in control for that. I mean, look at her, all neatly made up for some work-related conference she was going to later. On a Saturday, for God's sake. I could see she'd made a particular effort too – lipliner as well as lipstick, and was that a new eyeshadow?

'Some new bloke started at work recently?' I said.

Mum's cheeks pinked under their dusting of powder. 'As a matter of fact, yes,' she said. 'He's nice. Divorced. Two young children, one of them Stone's age.'

I grinned.

'What?' she said.

'That sounded funny,' I said. 'Stone's age. Stone Age. Get it?'

Mum frowned. 'Anyway, we were talking about *you*,' she said. 'Why you're so quiet. Holed up in your room all the time.' She put her arm round my shoulders and hugged me. 'Is it a boy you've met doing the play?'

I pulled away. Mum was always doing this, trying to get me to talk to her about private stuff. I still hadn't told anyone how Flynn had made me feel. What was the point? I was a zillion miles from ever getting to know him better. He was far too attractive and sure of himself to be interested in someone like me. If I told anyone they'd just feel sorry for me or – worse – start offering me advice.

'Come on, Riv,' Mum wheedled. 'We used to talk all the time.'

This was true. When I was younger, after Dad left, I remember clinging to Mum like I was falling out of an aeroplane and she was the parachute. I told her everything that was happening at school. What I did. Who was friends with whom. Everything the teachers said.

And then, one day, when I was thirteen, Dad took me and Stone to meet his new girlfriend. Gemma. She was younger than Mum, with long black hair down to her waist and a dreamy look in her eye – a sort of anti-Mum. Or maybe just more like how Mum used to be.

Dad and Gemma were living together on a commune – growing organic vegetables and working the land and stuff. It was what Dad had wanted to do for ages – but Mum always ridiculed it as impractical and childish.

Anyway, after I met Gemma, I didn't feel the same about Mum any more. I could see how happy Gemma and their life together made Dad. And it made me feel angry – like it was all Mum's fault for not being who Dad needed her to be.

'What about your friends, then,' Mum said, leaning back in her chair and studying my face. 'Have you fallen out with Emmi? Or Grace?'

I shook my head. *God*. Couldn't she see I didn't want to talk?

But Mum just sat there, staring at me. I was going to have to say something, just to get rid of her.

I took a deep breath. 'I wish I was playing Juliet,' I said.

This was true, though it wasn't the reason why I'd spent so much time in my room recently.

Mum smiled triumphantly, clearly thinking she'd cracked me.

'Darling, don't be so silly,' she said. 'The Nurse is a great part. A character part. *Far* more interesting than drippy Juliet.'

'I don't think Juliet's drippy,' I said, feeling angry.

Mum rolled her eyes. 'I just mean that she spends the whole play mooning over a boy, and then tops herself because she thinks he's dead. It's hardly a great feminist example, is it?'

I swallowed. I really didn't want to get into this with Mum. But a small part of me wanted to yell at her: *Who cares if it's not feminist? It's about dying for love! Isn't love the most important thing in the world?*

54

Instead I got up and grabbed my copy of the play off the table.

'No, Mum, it's not a feminist example, but then it's not supposed to be – it's not a feminist play,' I said curtly.

I stalked out of the kitchen and went up to my room.

I headed off to the High Street soon afterwards. I was meeting up with Emmi and Grace in a local café, then we were going into town to look seriously for shoes. Well, Emmi was going to look seriously for shoes. In practice, Grace would try loads on and sigh a lot about how hard it is for her to find shoes that fit her tiny feet. As for me, I know it's practically heresy to say this, but I actually find shopping for clothes and shoes quite boring. I go cos it's what girls do. And Emmi makes it fun by encouraging us to try on outrageous clothes and jewellery. But I hardly ever buy anything. Unlike Emmi, who's loaded and has a wardrobe bigger than a double-decker bus.

It was warmer outside than I'd realised and, as I strolled the ten-minute walk to the shops, I took off my jacket. I was wearing quite a tight-fitting top underneath. It didn't used to be tight, but I guess it shrank in the wash.

I hoped it had shrunk, anyway. The alternative was too depressing to consider.

Several guys stared at me as I turned onto the High Street. I hate that, men gawping at my boobs. I shook out my jacket and held it up to slide my arm through. Better to be hot than stared at.

And then I saw him. Flynn. Sauntering down the hill towards me. He hadn't seen me. He was busy chatting. *Oh God*. He was chatting to a girl. I stood rigid, the jacket still held out in front of me.

She was gorgeous. Tall – almost as tall as him – with a mass of dark red hair and a slim, sinewy body.

They were both wearing jeans. Hers were fastened by one of those incredibly trendy belts everyone wears nowadays. He had on a faded green T-shirt. She was smiling at him, laughing at something he'd said.

My heart seemed to shrink, cold, down into my stomach. I felt like crying. He was looking around now. Glancing at a girl passing by in a short skirt. Then he dipped his head, his fringe flopping gorgeously over one eye, and he checked his watch. He said something to the red-haired girl beside him. She nodded.

As they drew closer, I could see their faces more clearly. Hers was elegant and refined-looking. She had a long, slender nose that sloped up at the end, just like his.

I sighed, remembering something Emmi had told me about people being attracted to people who looked like them.

At the time I'd thought it was rubbish.

They were only about twenty metres away from me now. They were going to pass me in less than a minute. What should I do?

Part of me wanted to scurry away across the road. But a larger – a much larger – part of me wanted to walk up to him and say 'Hi'.

I could make it casual. I mean, what was the big deal about just saying 'Hi'? We were in a play together after all. And I had to know how he felt about her. So far he hadn't touched her. Maybe, just maybe – though looking at how beautiful she was I was crazy to even hope it – they were only friends.

The seconds ticked past. Flynn and the girl drew nearer.

I made my decision. I was going to walk past, looking at him.

If he looked up and noticed me, I'd say 'Hi'. If he didn't, I'd walk on and say nothing.

I set off, my jacket limp in my hand, my heart pounding in my chest.

57

7

I was only dimly aware of the other shoppers around me. Several mothers with kids in buggies. A small knot of teenage boys lounging against a boarded-up shop, sharing a fag. An elderly lady pulling a shopping trolley.

As I drew closer to Flynn, they faded into the background, along with the smell of traffic fumes and the sounds of cars and people talking. I fixed my eyes intently on him. Surely if I stared at him hard enough, he'd see me? But he didn't. He didn't. We were two metres away from each other. A metre. Less.

And then he looked up.

I stopped instantly. Despite having been preparing for this moment for the whole of the last minute, I felt shocked. Dizzy, almost, at the intense, searching way he stared into my eyes.

Flynn took a step on, still staring at me, then he

stopped too. Beside him the red-haired girl shuffled impatiently.

'Hi.' *Jeez*, I sounded as if I was being strangled.

Flynn narrowed his eyes slightly. 'River?' He grinned.

I nodded idiotically. His smile was sending my insides into somersaults. I gripped my jacket tighter.

'What are you doing here?' Flynn said.

'I live round the corner,' I stammered. 'I was . . . I was just out.'

I didn't want to mention the fact that I was meeting Emmi and Grace.

There was a pause. The red-haired girl tugged on Flynn's arm. But he was still looking at me.

'Er . . . what about you?' I said, forcing a smile. 'This isn't near your school.'

'No.' Flynn ran his hand through his hair. He glanced sideways at the redhead. 'I'm walking Siobhan down to her new job – a hair salon that's just opened down the Broadway. I've gotta go too so I know where it is, when I pick her up.'

I could feel the smile freezing on my face. Friends didn't pick each other up after work.

'Oh,' I said, looking down. 'Right, well . . .'

'D'you want to come with us?' Flynn said. 'It's not far, is it, Siob?'

Siobhan's beautiful green eyes widened with

what I took to be a look of hostile alarm. 'No,' she said slowly. 'But we have to go now. I don't want to be late.'

We set off, Flynn in the middle, explaining to Siobhan that he knew me from the play at school.

I was completely bewildered. What was he doing, inviting me to walk with him and his girlfriend when she was clearly so uncomfortable about it? Siobhan kept her eyes lowered, avoiding looking straight at me. A minute later and we arrived outside a smart-looking hair salon with the words *Goode's Hair Days* printed in black across the top.

'See you at six,' Flynn said.

Siobhan nodded, mumbled a miserable-sounding goodbye, then slipped through the front door of the shop.

Flynn turned to me and grinned again. 'D'you wanna get a coffee?' he said.

I blinked at him, utterly confused. Could he not see how annoyed Siobhan had been? 'Er . . .'

The smile fell from Flynn's face. He stared at me for a second, then he scowled.

'No problem.' He swung away from me and took a long stride back up the High Street.

I stared at him in horror. Then I practically flew the two-metre gap that had already opened up between us.

'I do,' I said breathlessly, falling into a rapid walk beside him. 'Want to get a coffee, I mean. It's just.' I nodded back towards the hair salon. 'Won't *she* mind?'

Flynn frowned. 'Siobhan? Why should she? She's so nervous about her new job I doubt if . . .' He stopped, his face splitting into an enormous grin. His eyes shone – more green than gold in the harsh sunlight. 'Er . . . Siobhan's my sister,' he said.

He was still grinning as we walked into the little café two doors back up the High Street. It was crowded with Saturday shoppers. Bulging plastic bags filled the floor between each of the cramped tables.

I followed Flynn over to the counter. My face was burning with embarrassment. It wasn't just that I'd got their relationship all wrong – *for goodness' sake, River, no wonder their noses looked alike* – it was the fact that by drawing attention to it, I'd implied that Flynn inviting me for a coffee somehow meant something. Like a date. When to him it was probably just a friendly gesture.

I took a deep breath, trying to calm down. I gazed at the rows of cakes and buns behind the glass casing above the counter. Out of the corner of my eye I could see Flynn pulling money out of his jeans pocket. He tipped all the coins into one hand and started counting them with the forefinger of the other. Three pound coins, three fifty-pence pieces and a bunch of tens and twenties.

'Don't worry,' I smiled. 'I've got plenty of cash.'

Flynn stared up at me, the grin completely gone from his face. His lips were pressed together in a thin line, his eyes flashing with anger.

'I'm fine,' he snapped. 'It's sorted.'

He glared at me, as if challenging me to disagree.

My heart thudded. I looked away. What was his problem? I remembered how angry he'd looked when he'd caught me staring at his scuffed shoes and second-hand trousers back at that first rehearsal.

'River?'

I looked up. The anger had gone from his eyes, but he was still looking at me intently. I got that hot, powerful feeling of wanting him so badly that my legs nearly gave way. But this time I didn't trust it. I didn't trust him.

'You can even have a piece of cake if you want.' He smiled weakly, holding out his palm to show me how much money was on it.

I shook my head.

There was an awkward silence as we shuffled to the head of the queue and Flynn asked for two cappuccinos. Large ones.

As we fought our way through the crowded shop

to a small table near the window, I started to feel angry.

We sat down. Flynn took a gulp of his coffee. I sat back and folded my arms.

'That was really rude,' I said. 'The way you spoke to me.'

His eyes darted up, a look of surprise on his face.

'I know.' He looked away. 'I'm sorry.'

He took another gulp of coffee. I looked at his T-shirt more closely. It wasn't just faded. It was all pulled out of shape at the bottom – like things get when you've washed them too much. His jeans were the same. A good make, but frayed and worn. These clothes were as second-hand as his school uniform.

He still looked good in them, but they were undeniably cheap.

'Why d'you care so much about not having any money?' I said.

Flynn looked at me again. His expressive face told me quite clearly that he was staggered at my asking such a brazen question.

I was pretty staggered at myself. But there was something about Flynn that made me feel reckless. I mean, he was so open. So direct. Why shouldn't I be?

Flynn put down his coffee mug and sat back in his chair.

'Obviously you do have money,' he said. 'Or else you wouldn't ask such a frigging stupid question.'

My heart pounded. We stared at each other for a long moment. It was like being locked in a cage with a lion. Terrifying. But exhilarating to be up close to something so powerful.

'I don't have that much money,' I said defensively.

Flynn snorted. 'I bet you even get an allowance,' he said.

'So what?' I said, jutting out my chin. 'That wasn't a crime last time I checked.'

Flynn's face dissolved into another smile. It was like seeing the sun come out after a storm. 'You're a bold piece,' he said, grinning more deeply. 'A bold piece. That's what my mum would say, anyway.'

I grinned back, relieved.

'Have you got any other brothers or sisters?' I said. 'Apart from Siobhan.'

Flynn nodded. 'I've got a younger sister too,' he said.

I sat forward, transfixed by his eyes, by the elegant slope of his nose, by the perfect curve of his lips. 'I've got a younger brother,' I said. 'Stone. He doesn't talk much. In fact he's a pig, mostly, but . . .' I stopped.

An incredulous expression had spread over

Flynn's face. 'You have a brother called *Stone*?' he said.

I could feel a red flush creeping up round my neck. I hate it when people take the mickey out of our names. I mean, it's not our fault Mum and Dad spent the whole of the nineties smoking pot and demonstrating against GM foods.

I shrugged, staring down at the table and cupping my mug in my hands. One of Flynn's strong fingers pressed against my hand. The touch of it was like a burn.

I looked up at him.

'Sorry. Again,' he mouthed.

We stared at each other for a moment. Then I sipped at my coffee, trying desperately to think of something to say.

'Your sister's very pretty,' I said. 'Beautiful, actually.'

'Yeah?' Flynn looked mildly surprised. 'Really?'

I nodded. 'Her hair's amazing. And she's got a great figure.'

Flynn screwed up his face. 'You're not a lesbian, are you?'

'No,' I said indignantly, feeling myself blushing again. 'Not that there's anything wrong with being gay, but no.'

Flynn laughed. 'Good,' he said. 'That would be just my luck.'

My breath caught in my throat as his eyes rested on mine again.

Saying that . . . that meant he was interested, didn't it? That definitely implied he was interested.

Flynn was still staring at me. Into me.

And then my phone buzzed.

I leaped about ten centimetres in the air, then pulled my mobile out of my trouser pocket. My blush deepened as I bent over the text message. How seriously uncool was it to jump when your own phone rang?

Whre r u? G & me gng 2 look @ shop, bttm Brdwy. Wl go alone if u nt here in 2 . . . hurry up! x

Emmi. I'd completely forgotten I was supposed to meet her and Grace further up the High Street half an hour ago.

Oh no. They were going to be walking down to the bottom of the Broadway. They'd pass right by this café. I looked around. We were sitting beside the window and all the other tables were full.

If Emmi and Grace looked into the café and saw me with Flynn . . .

I couldn't face it. This thing with Flynn was all so uncertain. So fragile. And my feelings were so confusing. No way was I ready to tell Emmi and Grace about it. Not until I was more sure of how I felt. Right now it was private – it belonged to me and him.

No one else.

Flynn raised his eyebrows. 'Who was that?'

I shook my head. 'No one,' I said. I didn't want to tell him I was supposed to be meeting Emmi and Grace. He might suggest he came along to say hello or something.

I stood up. 'I gotta go,' I said. 'I'm meeting someone.'

Flynn stood up too. *God*. He was so much taller than me. I felt suddenly ridiculous, only coming up to his chest like I did. I glanced up at him. For the first time since I'd met him he looked unsure of himself, like he didn't know what to say or do next.

'Thanks for the coffee,' I said. My mouth felt dry. I didn't want to go. But Emmi and Grace would be down here any second.

I turned and practically raced out of the coffee shop.

8

I spent the rest of the weekend reliving what had happened in the coffee shop. Thinking about Flynn.

I could feel myself falling for him. It was the weirdest sensation, like the thought of him was sucking me in – taking up all my energy.

I couldn't believe I still knew so little about him. OK, so I was pretty sure he wasn't well off and I knew he had a couple of sisters, but that was about it. Discovering those things had only thrown up far more interesting questions, none of which I had satisfactory answers to.

Why was he so angry about being poor? Loads of people don't have much money, but Flynn acted like it was . . . I dunno . . . somehow shameful.

And why was he so protective of his sister? It struck me when I thought about it that it was extremely odd for him to pick her up after work. I mean, she was older than him, and he was in the sixth form: one year older than me. That meant she must be at least eighteen. Surely she could get herself home after work on her own?

I tossed and turned, unable to sleep on Sunday night. If only I'd been able to stay longer at the café, I might have worked some of it out. We could have talked about the play too. I could have found out why Flynn had said it was great that I wasn't Catholic. Why he didn't like anyone using his first name, Patrick.

I could have given him the chance to ask for my phone number.

Jeez. I could have asked him for his.

Instead, I'd met up with Emmi and Grace and had another coffee with them, then we'd set off for town, where – true to form – Emmi had spent her allowance on three pairs of outrageously sexy heels and Grace had deliberated for half an hour over a new pair of trainers.

Part of me wanted to talk to them about Flynn. I knew if it was either of them, they would have gone on and on about him. In fact, Grace did go on and on about Darren. While Emmi let slip – very casually, as if she wasn't that bothered – that Alex had asked her to some party a week next Saturday.

But I couldn't do it. Not just because of how

uncertain everything was with Flynn, but because of how powerfully I felt about him.

How deep my wanting him went.

I approached Monday's rehearsal in a state of high excitement. Surely Flynn was bound to say something to me today?

But he wasn't there. And this time James had no reason to offer up.

Bitterly disappointed, I schlepped moodily home with Emmi and Grace afterwards. They were both buzzing from the rehearsal, which had gone well, despite Flynn's absence.

'Wasn't it funny when Mr Nichols got Alex to do that sword fight with a folded-up piece of paper?' That was Emmi.

Grace giggled. 'Yeah. His face when it flopped over that time.'

She and Emmi clutched their mouths, remembering.

'I thought it was stupid doing the fight without Romeo being there,' I said grumpily.

Emmi and Grace exchanged glances.

'I thought it was better without him,' Emmi said, looking at me strangely. 'He's a bit weird if you ask me. You know. Intense.'

I shrugged. 'I guess,' I said.

'And he always looks so angry,' Grace added. 'To be honest, sometimes he frightens me.'

'Oh, for goodness sake, Grace,' Emmi laughed. 'You get scared over nothing. He's just a bit weird. He's not even that good-looking.'

I sat back, more glad than ever that I hadn't said anything to them about my feelings for Flynn.

Flynn was at the next rehearsal – we were having two a week now, after school on Mondays and Thursdays. It was October – nearly half-term – and the play was going to be performed the week before the end of term – the middle of December.

Mr Nichols spent the first ten minutes of our rehearsal time trying to impress upon us the importance of learning our lines over half-term and threatening to up the rehearsals to every night during November.

I tried to catch Flynn's eye while he was speaking, but failed. Flynn simply stared stonily down at his script the whole time Mr Nichols was talking. He didn't look at me once during the whole of the rehearsal either. And he didn't come down to the common room afterwards for the orange juice. My stomach was in knots. Why had he changed? I was sure he'd been interested in me when we were having our coffee. Why was he ignoring me now? Had I done something to annoy him?

The following week I wasn't called for the Monday rehearsal, but the same thing happened on the Thursday. Flynn completely ignored me. I was beside myself. I couldn't work out what I'd done.

I started dreaming about him. Long, slow dreams in which he paced around me like a lion, getting closer and closer and finally reaching out to hold me, to kiss me. I would wake up sweating. Unable to sleep. Unable to get him out of my head.

Emmi insisted Grace and I came to the party Alex had invited her to. It was over in Stoke Newington. I agreed with Mum that the three of us would get the night bus back together and sleep over at mine. That meant she didn't mind us getting back late – up to 1 a.m.

The others brought their stuff over to my house early. We set out the camp beds in my room and then took ages getting ready. We did each other's nails and hair and tried on various outfits. Emmi was in a skin-tight dress and a pair of the killer heels she'd bought two weeks before. I knew from the glint in her eye that Alex was definitely going to get lucky tonight. But she didn't talk about him at all.

Instead, our conversation revolved around Grace's Darren.

'He's okay,' Grace said unenthusiastically, 'but I'm starting to think he's a bit boring.'

Emmi and I exchanged 'we could have told you *that*' glances, then Emmi persuaded Grace to wear this cropped, strappy top. It wasn't Grace at all – though she looked great in it. I could see Emmi was planning to launch Grace at one of Alex's unsuspecting friends. She loves it when we go out with guys who get on – all the double-date possibilities seem to give her a massive thrill. Just the idea of them.

'What are you wearing, River?' Emmi said, looking up from Grace's hair, a section of which she was now teasing into a line of blonde mini-plaits.

'Just this, I guess,' I said, indicating my old jeans and the pale blue sleeveless top I was wearing.

'No way.' Emmi plumped up her hair like she meant business. She rummaged through my wardrobe then appeared with a low-cut black top with little spaghetti straps and a ruchy bit under the boobs. 'You have to wear this,' she said. 'It'll make your tits look amazing.'

I stared at her. I'd bought that top on a whim weeks ago. I loved it, but whenever I put it on I always felt too big. Too exposed.

'Everyone'll stare at me,' I said.

'So?' Emmi rolled her eyes. 'That's the point, isn't it? At least you've got something to stare at.'

'But River wants love,' Grace giggled. 'Not boys staring at her chest.'

Emmi snorted. 'You won't get one without the other,' she said flatly. 'Put it on.'

In the end, I put it on, but took my jacket too. If I felt too self-conscious, I could always put the jacket on top. Well, that's what I told myself. Underneath, I was hoping the top really did make me look good, and thinking that I'd only put the jacket on over it if Flynn wasn't there.

As we traipsed downstairs, Stone was lingering in the hall. He was pretending to be reading a magazine, but I could see him sneaking long, lustful looks at Emmi while the three of us fussed and flapped at the door, putting on some last-minute lipgloss.

Creep, I thought. Then I remembered myself looking at Flynn in rehearsals and how it had felt when he'd stared back at me, and I blushed so deeply that both Grace and Emmi asked me if I was feeling all right.

9

It took ages to get to the party. I felt nervous as we walked in – wondering if . . . hoping . . . that Flynn was going to be here.

He wasn't.

It wasn't much of a party either. Rubbish music. Not that many people.

Alex whisked Emmi off almost as soon as we arrived. Seconds later James Malloy materialised beside me and Grace, a bunch of beer bottles in either hand. From the way he smiled at Grace, it was clear his fixation on Emmi had completely gone. He started chatting away with surprising confidence. I looked at Grace. Mmmn. Maybe it wasn't so surprising. She was blushing, smiling up at him coyly.

I didn't give much for Darren's chances of not getting dumped in the next twenty-four hours.

James didn't seem to know if Flynn was coming

or not. I drank a couple of beers too fast, out of nerves. Then, with no sign of Flynn in the house, and with Grace and James ignoring everyone else, I drank another out of boredom.

I'd just extricated myself from a long and tedious conversation with the red-haired boy who played Lord Capulet when Flynn finally turned up. It was almost eleven o'clock. I looked up and he was there, standing in the living room doorway. His white shirt was creased. He looked tired, but gorgeous.

I held my breath as he gazed round the room.

Notice me.

But his eyes skittered past me, as if he hadn't seen me. He looked down at the floor and shoved his hands in his pockets.

I glanced over at Grace. James was definitely moving in on her – she had her back against the living room wall and he was leaning his arm against it, above her head. Still, they weren't kissing yet.

I went over. 'Hey, James,' I said lightly.

He turned round.

'Flynn's here,' I said.

James showed absolutely no interest in this bit of information.

'Oh.' He turned back to Grace.

'How come he's so late?' I persisted.

This time James didn't even turn round. 'Just finished work, I expect.' He leaned closer to Grace and smiled down at her.

Work? What kind of work did Flynn do on a Saturday night? I stared across the room at him for a minute longer, then, emboldened by my three beers, I decided to go and talk to him. I set off across the carpet, but before I got halfway he caught my eye. I could see from his expression that he knew I was coming to speak to him. He turned away and vanished from the doorway.

I stopped, stock-still, in the middle of the carpet. It felt like a slap in the face. Why had he done that? Didn't he *want* to talk to me? Feeling utterly humiliated, I retraced my steps across the living room. James and Grace were now kissing.

Of course.

I wandered over to the kitchen where the music was louder and four boys were boasting loudly to each other about how much they'd drunk the night before.

I sidled across to the counter and helped myself to an open bottle. I didn't notice what was inside it – something pink and sweet. It tasted disgusting, but I didn't care. As I went back to the living room, tears welled up in my eyes. I took a few swigs from the bottle, then sank into the only available seat – at one end of a large, soft sofa. The boy at the other end squished up next to me.

'Hi there,' he slurred beerily.

I got up and took another swig from my bottle. Then several more. The bottle was almost empty now. A few hot, fat tears trickled down my face.

What a rubbish party. Boys all over Grace and Emmi. And me as unloved and unlovable as ever.

Another boy wandered over to me and offered me one of those premixed rum and juice drinks. I took the bottle, twisted off the cap and drained it fast. The boy started talking to me about some band I'd never heard of. *God*. Why were boys so boring?

After about fifteen minutes, I was feeling sick as well as bored. Making some excuse about needing a pee, I staggered out into the hall. Maybe some water on my face would help. I stumbled up the stairs in search of a bathroom.

I was swaying a little as I walked. About halfway up, I missed my footing and lurched over, onto the stair rail. A hand pressed into my back, steadying me.

'Doesn't your boyfriend mind you coming to parties and getting drunk?' said a familiar and very sarcastic voice.

I spun round, nearly losing my footing again.

Flynn was on the step beneath me, which put our heads at the same level. I stared at him, part of me soaking in the golden glow of his eyes, part of me furious at the contempt which dripped from his voice.

'I'm not drunk,' I slurred angrily. 'And I don't have a boyfriend.'

I turned away and strode haughtily up the rest of the stairs. I had to let go of the stair rail as I reached the landing – which immediately started to spin around me. My stomach clenched in a spasm of pain.

I put out my arm to steady myself. Flynn was still there. He caught my arm. 'Are you okay?' he said, more gently.

I swallowed. 'I'm fine,' I snapped. My stomach heaved. *Oh God.* 'Except . . . except I think I might be sick.'

Flynn pushed open the door in front of us. The bathroom. As he stood back to let me through, my gut spasmed with pain again. I stumbled inside, shoved at the door behind me and sank to my knees in front of the toilet. A few seconds later and my stomach was heaving itself up into the toilet bowl.

'Aahh,' I moaned to myself, tears welling in my eyes. My forehead felt clammy with sweat, my throat burnt and swollen. *Ugh*. Vomiting is so disgusting. It doesn't often happen . . . I mean, I can't remember when I was last ill . . . but when it does, I hate it . . .

A hand stroked my hair.

'AAH!' I jumped up, spinning round. Flynn was straightening up behind me. The bathroom door was shut behind him. *Oh my God*. He was in the room. He'd *been* in the room when . . . I stared up at him, speechless. I couldn't believe he'd just seen me puke my guts up. I turned quickly, put the toilet seat down and flushed.

'Better?' Flynn took a sip from his plastic cup. The liquid inside looked clear.

'You oughta be careful.' I forced a grin, trying to cover up just how hideously embarrassed I was. 'Neat vodka? You'll be next.'

He looked at me without smiling, then held out the cup. 'It's water,' he said. 'I don't drink alcohol.'

I stared at him in disbelief.

'Have it,' he said. 'I was going anyway.'

I took the cup from his hand and took a tiny sip. Water. It soothed the burning in my throat. I wanted to rinse my mouth out properly. But there was no way, not with Flynn watching.

Instead, I wiped my mouth with the back of my shaking hand, sank down on the floor and leaned against the side of the bath. At least I didn't feel sick any more.

Flynn towered over me. 'I wanted to make sure you were okay.'

He hesitated.

'Why don't you drink alcohol?' I said, fixated by this latest intriguing revelation.

Flynn shrugged, his mouth twisting into an ironic smile. 'Look where it gets you,' he said, indicating the toilet behind me.

I blushed. 'Okay, but . . . I mean, is it that you don't like the taste?'

'It's not that.' Flynn paused. Then he sat down on the floor opposite me. 'Er . . . did you mean . . . what you said, about not having a boyfriend?'

I frowned at him. My head felt clearer than it had, but not totally clear. Why on earth would he think I had a boyfriend?

'Yes,' I said.

Flynn stared at me. 'It's just, when I saw you, when we had that coffee . . . the way you rushed off after getting that phone call. I could see you didn't want whoever it was to know you were with me.' He shrugged. 'I kind of assumed it was some guy.'

I frowned. 'It was Emmi,' I said. 'Emmi and Grace. I was late meeting them. That was all.'

That wasn't quite all, of course. I hadn't wanted

81

them to see me with Flynn, but . . . Another thought occurred to me.

'Why didn't you ask me if I was going out with anyone?' I said.

Flynn shrugged again. He looked away.

He didn't ask because he likes you, you idiot. And he didn't want to risk being humiliated in case you said you were with someone else.

I chuckled drunkenly, suddenly feeling deliriously happy.

He likes me. He likes me.

Except. Except . . . My befuddled brain inched its way to the horrible truth of the situation. I was drunk and he was not only sober but actually *non-drinking* for some reason. Worse. *Oh God.* Worse of all possible worses. He'd just seen me be sick. Which must be the biggest turn-off known to mankind.

Flynn stood up and held out his hand. 'You should get some air,' he said.

I took his hand and let him pull me to my feet. He kept hold of my hand as we crossed the landing and went down the stairs. Outside the front of the house the street was quiet, just a steady *thump, thump* from the music inside.

As we walked a little way down the pavement, I shivered. *Damn*, I'd left my jacket inside. The cold air was sobering me up fast, though. I remembered how I'd cried before I'd puked and wished I'd looked in the bathroom mirror before I'd left the room.

Flynn was looking at me again. I turned my face away and licked at the finger of my free hand. I ran it desperately under my eyes, hoping I'd pick up any smudged traces of eyeliner and mascara.

Flynn took my arm and pulled me round. I was really shivering now. It was freezing with just the little black top on. He put his hands on my arms and rubbed them up and down. His eyes were dark gold now and soft in the street lamp above our heads.

'Why do you hate drinking so much?' I said slowly.

He stopped rubbing my arms and let his hands fall to his sides. 'I don't,' he said. 'I just hate drunks.'

A car whooshed past us. I didn't know what to say.

I only got drunk because you didn't look at me.

Flynn looked over my head into the night. Then he took a step back, away from me. 'Are you okay?' he said.

I nodded. 'Flynn?'

He raised his eyebrows.

'I . . . I like talking to you.' I closed my eyes. *How pathetic did I sound? Shut up, River. Shut up until you're sober.*

I felt his fingers draw gently down the side of my face.

83

I shivered, my skin tingling where he'd touched me. I looked up. He was staring at me, his expression somehow both tender and exasperated all at once.

My heart was pounding, my legs threatening to fall away from beneath me. *Kiss me. Kiss me.*

He leaned forward as if he was going to kiss me, then he whispered, 'I like you too, River, but I'm not kissing you while you're drunk and your mouth tastes of puke.'

He drew back and grinned. A confident, entirely sexy, beautiful grin. 'I'll walk you home, though,' he said. 'If you'd like?'

I blinked. *Oh yes, oh yes. I would like.*

Then I remembered.

'I can't,' I stammered. 'I'm supposed to be going back with Emmi and Grace later. They're sleeping over at my house.'

Flynn stared at me, his eyes boring right into me.

'I can't stay here any longer,' he said. 'Mum's working nights this week. I have to get back before twelve-fifteen or else Caitlin and Siobhan'll be on their own.'

I wanted to ask him why Siobhan couldn't look after Caitlin. Why she couldn't stay on her own. But his eyes were stripping me of the power of speech. Or maybe it was all the beer and rum.

'Promise me you'll go straight inside and find Grace and James,' Flynn said. 'Tell James I want him to take you home, to make sure you get back all right. And promise me you'll go soon. Okay?'

I nodded. He pointed towards the house. 'I'll watch you back inside. Go on.'

I walked carefully back along the pavement, feeling ridiculously happy. At the door I turned. Flynn was still watching me. He raised his hand in a wave, then spun round, shoved his hands in his pockets and vanished into the night.

10

I went straight up to Grace and James when I got back to the party. They were all over each other. I had to stand right next to them for about ten seconds before they even saw me.

'I've just been sick,' I said.

'Oh, Riv.' Grace made a sympathetic face. But I could see she was in no mood to leave. James said nothing. I turned to him.

'Flynn saw me being ill. He's gone, but he said I should ask you . . .' I stopped. Apart from not really wanting to talk about Flynn in front of Grace, it struck me that there was really no need for James to come home with us at all. Emmi, Grace and I were perfectly capable of making our own way back.

But James was already nodding. 'He wants me to take you home? That's fine,' he said.

'What?' Grace was looking at him, horrified.

'Both of you, I mean,' James said hastily.

Grace frowned. 'Are you really feeling ill, Riv?'

I swallowed. I wasn't too bad, not any more. But I'd promised Flynn I'd let James make sure I got back okay. And I'd said I'd leave soon. I frowned. Something about the leaving soon thing didn't quite make sense, though I couldn't put my finger on what.

'Grace, why don't you find Emmi? Tell her River's not well. Needs to go,' James said quickly. 'I'll get her a drink of water.'

Grace looked at him, then nodded. She disappeared out of the room. As soon as she was gone, James grabbed my arm. 'Are you sure you're okay?'

I stared at him. 'I'm fine, look, Flynn was just suggesting you might take me home. He wanted me to go soon. But there's no need – I feel okay now. And I'll be with Emmi and Grace when I do leave.'

James shook his head. 'He'll be really annoyed at me if I don't do what he said. Anyway,' his face reddened, 'Grace is staying with you, isn't she?'

I frowned. 'How d'you mean, "really annoyed at you"? Why would he be? I don't understand.'

'Me and Flynn have an agreement. He lets me copy his English and history homework. Then, if he asks me to do something like this, I do it. No questions.'

My frown deepened. 'How often does he ask you to walk his . . . his friends home?'

'He hasn't before. But sometimes he asks me to meet his sister from work. If he has to be somewhere else. Once I was late and he was so mad, I thought he was going to hit me.'

'Why does he always meet his sister?' I said.

James shrugged. 'Dunno. He's never said. He only says that he has to look after her.' He paused, blushing again. 'Look. It's no big deal,' he said.

'Okay,' I said slowly, my mind whirling. Why was Flynn so protective of his sister? And why, now, was . . .

'Why's he doing this for me?' I said.

'He's probably worried about you going home drunk,' James said. 'He's got a massive thing about alcohol. All drugs, but alcohol especially. Never touches it.'

'I know,' I said. 'What's that about?'

James shrugged again. 'No idea. But I've never seen him have so much as a sip of beer and he gets really angry if you push him on it.'

I frowned. The list of things which made Flynn really angry was getting longer every time I met him. Money. Drugs. Booze. People turning up late to protect his sister from some mysterious danger.

I spotted Grace – minus Emmi, but carrying both our jackets in her arms – appearing at the doorway.

'Okay,' I whispered, remembering what hadn't

made sense to me before. 'I see why he wants you to make sure I get home all right, but why did he say I should go soon? Wouldn't it make more sense for me to sit here quietly for a bit until I felt properly better?'

I stared at James, wondering what new revelation I was going to get about Flynn's personality now.

James's blush deepened. 'Er . . .' he said, watching Grace wander over to us. 'I imagine that's just because he doesn't want you getting with anyone else.'

The next day was Sunday. Stone and I went to see Dad at his commune. I hardly spoke all the way there. My head was full of Flynn and the night before.

Part of me was mortified that he'd seen me drunk and puking. But part of me kept remembering the way he'd looked at me – and how he'd said he liked me too . . .

This last point was reinforced by James. He'd spent most of the journey wrapped around Grace and, at some point, had mentioned to her that he thought Flynn was interested in me. Grace had pestered me all night for details. I kept insisting nothing had happened between me and Flynn. Which was true. We hadn't even kissed.

I just said he'd been nice about me being sick and I couldn't really remember the rest of it.

Emmi had refused to come home with us. Grace and I agreed to tell my mum she'd decided to go back to hers instead. She turned up the next morning to pick up her stuff – explaining in graphic detail how she'd spent the whole night with Alex.

I could tell she wasn't pleased when Grace told her about me and Flynn.

'He's a bit weird, Riv,' she said. 'Don't you think? Dead intense. I mean, look at last night. He wasn't even there and he got the three of you to do what he wanted and go straight home.'

I shrugged. 'He was just trying to be nice,' I said. But some part of me knew Emmi was right. It was a bit weird how protective he'd suddenly got. As if we'd been going out for ages or something. As if I was really important to him.

But then, I sighed, that was what made Flynn so amazing – how intense he was. How deeply I felt it all.

The day at the commune passed very slowly. Stone had a great time, helping Dad and Gemma dig potatoes. He still loves all that nature stuff, so long as he's sure his friends can't see him. I poked around, pretending to be working, but my heart wasn't in it.

Dad must've seen I wasn't enjoying myself. Not that I ever do, that much, at the commune. It's basically just a bunch of fields and huts – with a big old farmhouse in the middle. It's not that far out of London, but far enough to feel like the countryside.

Today I was so distracted I spent half my time outside just leaning on my fork, staring across the vegetable field towards the trees that marked a boundary with the row of houses next to the commune.

'What's the matter?' Dad said, coming up to me. I blushed. I'd just been remembering how Flynn had dragged his fingers slowly down my cheek. Dad grinned. 'Worried you broke a nail?'

I shook my head. I wasn't in the mood to be teased. Dad tilted his head to one side and smiled gently at me. 'Trouble shared, trouble halved,' he said.

Dad's full of cheesy old sayings like that. He's so laid-back nowadays he's practically asleep. He'd grown a bit of a beard since I'd last seen him two weeks ago, and there were lines round his eyes from all the squinting against the sun he does with his outdoor work.

'I guess commune-living seems pretty boring to you,' Dad said, still smiling that slow smile.

I shrugged.

He leaned forward on his fork, next to mine. 'What's on your mind, River?'

He stood there, silently, waiting for me to speak. I looked away, over at the trees again. It was a dull, cloudy day. Not all that cold for the middle of October, but grey, like it might rain later. The air felt heavy, oppressive. Somehow it reminded me of Flynn. Of the way his presence changed everything in a room.

Dad stood there, next to me, still waiting.

Mum would have jumped in by now. Emmi and Grace would never have shut up in the first place. It was easy not telling them how I felt. They never really listened anyway. But Dad was different. Since he'd been at the commune, he'd grown quieter and more determined, like he had this strong sense of who he was and what he wanted. Like he belonged.

The wind was rushing through the trees, sweeping my hair across my face. I hooked it back behind my ear, then turned to him.

'I met someone, Dad,' I said.

Dad gave a tiny nod. He didn't say anything.

'I really like him.' My cheeks felt hot, despite the chill of the wind. I looked down at my fork, at the rusty prongs, half covered with earth.

There was a long pause. Then Dad cleared his throat.

'How does he feel about you?'

I shrugged. 'I think he likes me. We haven't really gone out yet, but . . .' I prodded the fork into the ground. I could feel Dad's eyes watching me. 'Dad, I really like him but there are things about him I don't understand, like, he gets really angry about not having any money and he's really protective about his sister, and Emmi and Grace think he's weird cos he's so intense, but . . .'

I wanted to tell Dad how it felt when Flynn looked at me, how scary and powerful my feelings were, but there are some things you just can't say to your own father.

Dad sighed. 'You can never fully understand another person, River,' he said softly. 'Not really. Even here, at the commune, where we're all trying to be awake to the universe, we can't get away from it – the politics, the emotional baggage, the petty squabbles that stop us seeing each other clearly.' He put his rough, blistered hand on my shoulder. 'And it's normal for young men to be angry about things,' he said. 'I was. Still am when I see all the injustice and cruelty that goes on.'

I bent over and started digging again. Dad joined in. After a couple of minutes he straightened up and smiled at me.

'I wish, more than anything, your mum would have agreed to you growing up here,' he said. 'It's such a good grounding for dealing with outside life.'

I shook my head.

'Seriously, River . . .'

But before Dad could say anything else, Stone raced over to show us a weirdly-shaped potato he'd found.

'There's a whole bunch of them,' Stone said, looking like three years had just dropped off his age.

Dad laughed and went over to see for himself. I kept on digging with my fork, hitting a potato almost immediately. As I freed the earth around it, I thought about what Dad had said. Was it really true that you could never completely know another person? Surely that was what being in love meant – that you had that connection, that deep understanding.

I was sure Dad was wrong about other things too – how could living in a commune help you deal with real life? I mean, if I lived in a commune, how would I ever have met Flynn?

I sighed, then bent down and picked up the potato.

11

The next day, after school, Grace, Emmi and I went over to St Cletus's on the bus. Emmi made sarcastic remarks about me and Flynn all the way there.

'You can do way better than him, Riv,' she kept saying. 'I mean, have you seen his school uniform? It looks about tenth-hand.'

'River thinks that's romantic,' Grace said slyly. 'A poor man, nothing to give her but love.' She clasped her hands together and batted her eyelashes stupidly.

'Shut up, both of you,' I snarled.

They laughed. Emmi prodded me in the ribs. 'We're just teasing, girl,' she said. 'Flynn's okay, if you must. I mean, he *is* a bit weird. Way too intense for me – all that ridiculous *I must make sure you get home safely* nonsense. But he's obviously really clever and, anyway, loads of people go for that brooding thing he does.'

I rolled my eyes. She was making it sound like it was some kind of act that Flynn put on.

'Tell you one thing, though,' Emmi said, lowering her voice. 'He'll be after sex on your first date.'

Grace giggled.

I stared at Emmi, speechless.

'You can see it in his eyes,' she said mysteriously. 'He's not used to waiting for things.'

She sat back and started asking Grace what James Molloy was like as a kisser. I watched Grace go pink, admitting he was really quite good. And that she was definitely dumping Darren for him.

What on earth was Emmi going on about? Flynn and I hadn't even kissed yet and we'd met weeks ago. The last thing Flynn was, was pushy. I shook my head. It might all be about sex for Emmi, but the connection I'd felt with Flynn was different.

The bus took ages to get to the school. In the end we arrived ten minutes late for rehearsal. It was the last week before half-term and Mr Nichols was in full flow as we arrived in the rehearsal room.

'Everyone must know their lines by the end of half-term,' he was saying, pacing across the room. 'We're going to begin blocking the play using the actual stage once we're back, and rehearsals will increase to three times a week.'

I looked round for Flynn. He was at the end of a

long row of desks, his arms folded. He looked up at Mr Nichols. His face was sulky and sullen.

'I can't do three times a week,' he said. 'As you already know, *sir*.'

He said the last word with such withering contempt, I was surprised Mr Nichols didn't give him detention on the spot.

Mr Nichols narrowed his eyes. 'I didn't say everyone would have to *attend* three times a week, Flynn . . .' He caught sight of me and the other girls hovering by the door. 'Oh, you're here. Good. Come in, girls. Now let's get straight into Act 3, Scene 3.'

Flynn acted better than ever that night. He was clearly in a bad mood, but he seemed to channel it all into his part. His Romeo snapped and hissed with fury at being banished after killing Tybalt. As usual, Mr Nichols spent very little time directing him. Flynn just didn't need it in the same way that everyone else did. He already moved and spoke completely naturally, making total sense of everything he said.

Soon we were at my own entrance. My legs shook as I walked over to him.

He kept his face hidden as we had our first exchange, then in a single move he leaped up and grabbed my arm.

'Spakest thou of Juliet? How is it with her?'

He walked me backwards, still gripping my arm. For a second I forgot we were acting. The passion in his eyes was totally genuine. I wasn't listening to his words, only to the rolling rhythm of the lines and the agony in his voice.

'Where is she? And how doth she? And what says
My conceal'd lady to our cancell'd love?'

It was impossible to believe he didn't mean it. Love and despair were etched all over his face. He was obsessed with Juliet. Desperate to know if she hated him for killing her cousin, Tybalt.

As I spoke my lines back: '*O, she says nothing, sir, but weeps and weeps . . .*' I was thinking how much I wanted him to feel that strongly about me. About us.

Later, in his scene with Juliet, he was calm and gentle. He gazed at Emmi as if she was the only person in the room. Jealousy seeped through me like poison. It suddenly occurred to me that he was going to have to kiss her – several times – in the course of the play. Not tonight, maybe, but at some point in the rehearsals they were going to have to do it. And then over and over again. And through three performances too.

I felt sick. My heart thudded horribly. It was impossible. I couldn't bear it. I couldn't watch him crooning over her any more.

I walked out of the rehearsal room and went to the bathroom, where I took several deep breaths.

I was just going to have to get my head around it. It wasn't his fault. Or hers. There were kisses in the stage directions.

I gritted my teeth. He *had* to ask me out. We had to have a chance to talk properly. To kiss. Maybe if we knew where we stood with each other, it wouldn't be so hard to see him with Emmi in the play.

I looked into the mirror. Same old swamp-features: dull, mud-coloured hair, boring, ditchwater eyes. But there was something different about my face. *God*, I was positively glowing with excitement at the thought of him. I blushed, realising how obvious it must look. Then I gritted my teeth again.

I didn't care if it was obvious. Flynn knew how I felt. He'd known at the party. And he liked me too. Didn't he?

The rehearsal ended soon after I got back. Flynn came over to me immediately. While everyone else filed out of the room he started chatting about the party, asking if I'd got back all right. It was small talk, I quickly realised, designed to keep us where we were until the room emptied.

At last Mr Nichols was bustling us out of the room. We followed him towards the door, waiting while he switched out the light. He ushered us towards the stairs, then hurried on ahead, distracted by a squabble that had broken out near the bottom.

As soon as he'd disappeared from view, Flynn grabbed my hand.

Silently he pulled me back along the corridor to the rehearsal room. We slipped inside. It was dark, but not completely. Lights from the front of the school and the street beyond cast a yellowy glow across the desks and the cracked lino floor. The whiteboard – lying propped up beside the door – shone like a mirror.

We stood facing each other. Flynn's eyes were pieces of gold, gleaming out of the shadowy lines of his face. My heart raced as he looked at me. And looked at me.

It was incredibly sexy, and deeply, deeply unnerving.

Go with it. Don't say anything.

Yeah, right.

'Why can't you do three rehearsals a week?' I heard myself squeaking.

'Interferes with my jobs,' Flynn said softly. His eyes didn't flicker away from mine. Not for a second.

'What jobs?' I said.

'Organic vegetable deliveries two, sometimes three nights a week. Car washing on Saturdays until four, then clearing tables at a café in the evening,' he said evenly. 'Plus cleaning up at Goldbar's on Sundays from ten till two.'

He was still holding my gaze – a lion, getting ready to pounce.

My whole body trembled.

I couldn't look away.

'When d'you get time to do homework?' I gasped.

Shut up, River. Stop talking.

'Sunday afternoons,' he said. 'And when I get home in the evening.' He took a step towards me. I could almost feel the air between us compressing and crackling into a zillion little sparks. 'I don't want to talk about homework,' he whispered.

I couldn't say anything any more. All my words were lodged in my throat. I closed my eyes, feeling his head leaning down towards me, moving closer and closer.

I gave myself up to the kiss. Soft and light and gentle. It melted through my body like butter.

'FLYNN?' Mr Nichols' shout echoed down the corridor towards us. 'RIVER?'

I pulled away, turning wildly to face the door. I dimly registered that Flynn was still standing where he'd kissed me. He hadn't reacted to Mr Nichols at all.

The door flung open. Mr Nichols' long, lean body

was silhouetted against the bright corridor light behind him.

He stared at us, his eyes widening. 'What are . . . ? Get out here!' he snapped.

I scurried, red-faced, to the door. I could hear Mr Nichols talking in low, intense tones at Flynn to *get a move on*. I couldn't hear what, if anything, Flynn said back.

I ran on ahead, fled down the stairs and burst into the common room. Only a small knot of boys were still there, plus Emmi and Grace. Daisy had already left.

I made straight for Emmi. She and Alex were standing with their arms round each other. Emmi raised her eyebrows as I walked up but, thankfully, said nothing.

Flynn strolled in about five minutes later, his face all sulky. He gulped down a juice, then turned, looking for me. His eyes called me over. I was there in seconds.

'What happened?' I breathed. I could still feel his kiss on my lips.

Flynn shrugged. His face in the overhead fluorescent light suddenly looking pale and tired. 'Nothing. The usual. Frigging teachers telling you what to do.' He curled his lip. 'Like it's a frigging crime to . . .'

He looked at me. Hesitated. For a second he

looked unsure of himself. 'I won't be here on Thursday,' he said. 'I have to work.'

I stared at him. Thursday was the last rehearsal before half-term. If we didn't arrange something now, we wouldn't see each other for two weeks.

Ask me out. Now. Do it.

The noise level in the room rose as people started shuffling about, picking up coats and bags.

My heart pounded.

Come on. Do it.

Flynn's face clouded over. Was he angry again? No. I frowned. It wasn't anger. Suddenly I realised. He was *embarrassed*.

My mouth practically dropped open. Flynn? Embarrassed?

'River,' Emmi yelled across the room. 'Time to go.'

I could hear her and some of the boys laughing.

Oh, shut up. Please. Just shut up.

Flynn's eyes narrowed. It was like he was forcing himself to look at me. 'Can I have your number?' he said.

He sounded cross. But I knew that he wasn't. I suddenly knew that he was just hideously embarrassed, because he really, really wanted my number and he didn't want me to see how much.

My grin almost split my face in two. 'Sure,' I said. 'Give me your mobile and I'll . . .'

The sentence died on my lips as I saw Flynn's eyes harden.

Damn. Stupid, stupid, River.

He probably couldn't afford a mobile phone.

'No. Wait.' Before he could say anything I darted across the room to my bag and yanked out my copy of the play and a pen. I dashed back to Flynn and scrawled my mobile number across the bottom of the back page.

As Emmi sauntered up, I tore it off and handed it to him. He pocketed it and walked out of the room without a word.

'Whoa, he looked moody,' Emmi said. 'Didn't even say goodbye. I tell you, Riv, you gotta watch him. I reckon he could get punchy.'

I shook my head. 'Flynn's not like that,' I said. 'Honest, Emmi, you don't know him.'

I was expecting Emmi to turn round and point out that I barely knew him either, but I guess I must have sounded super-confident or something, because, for once, Emmi said nothing.

12

I waited three agonising days for him to phone. I stopped eating. I stopped sleeping. I kept my mobile charged and never more than a metre away from me.

He didn't call and he didn't call and he didn't call.

Emmi – who had of course seen me give him my number – asked what was going on. At first I tried to pretend we were just going to meet up to talk about the play. But Emmi saw through that straight away. So I fessed up.

I desperately needed to tell someone. And Emmi – despite her cynical attitude to boys and dating – was the best person. She might not understand Flynn. But she had more experience than anyone else I knew. And I knew I could trust her advice.

'Be cool,' she said. 'If he's interested, he'll ring.'

I didn't think it was that simple. I knew he was interested. He'd shown me that several times. But for Flynn there was more at stake. It had something to do with his anger. His pride. I didn't understand it, but I knew it was there.

He called, finally, after the Thursday evening rehearsal, which – as he'd explained – he'd had to miss.

'Hi,' he said.

My stomach flipped over at the sound of his voice.

'Hi,' I said, trying to sound casual. 'Finished delivering vegetables?'

'Yeah.' He sounded exhausted. 'Frigging ridiculous people – d'you know how much these organic things cost?'

As a matter of fact, I did know. Dad's commune was one of the places that supplied the local organic veg wholesalers with their produce. He often commented on how he hated it being so expensive, saying in the next breath how the additional cost was justified by the extra work put into growing the food.

'Still, it's worth paying more for healthier food,' I said hopefully.

Flynn snorted down the phone. 'If you can afford to pay more,' he said.

There was a short silence.

'So, d'you wanna meet up at the weekend?' he said.

'Sure.' My mouth was dry.

'Maybe we could go for coffee again?' he said. 'On Sunday?'

'Okay,' I said. 'The same place?'

'I was thinking the park,' Flynn said. 'Priory Park. That little café'll still be open. It said when I looked last week. Open through half-term. D'you wanna meet there? Say at three?'

'Sure.'

We didn't talk much after that. It was too awkward. But I didn't care. I had what I wanted. I had A Date.

A First Date.

I spent ages deciding what to wear. I hadn't intended to ask Emmi and Grace for advice but, in the end, I had to tell them I was seeing Flynn – Emmi was asking me every hour if he'd called. Anyway, from there it was a short step to the inevitable discussion about clothes and make-up.

Grace was all for looking outdoorsy and healthy. 'Jeans, trainers and just a smudge of lipgloss,' she said. 'The natural look.'

I didn't think so. Grace got away with that kind of look far better than me. She had pretty, regular features and an innocent air about her. I'd look like an elephant in jeans and trainers with no eye make-up.

'Something sexy,' Emmi advised. As she would.

'But not tarty. He's going to be all over you like a rash as it is.'

She told me to wear my black, ruchy top again. There was no way. Not to meet someone during the day.

In the end I settled on jeans and a soft, slightly fitted top. The top was quite smart, but the jeans would stop it looking too dressed up. And it was pale blue – which brought out the only latent colour in my boringly grey eyes.

I was planning on wearing my jacket too, but when Saturday arrived it was ridiculously warm. No wind at all, plus brilliant sunshine. I took my jacket anyway. I needed to know I could cover up if I wanted.

The café was crowded when I got there. I couldn't see Flynn anywhere. I'd deliberately – on Emmi's advice – arrived late. It was almost three-fifteen. He should be here. He should be here. Where was he?

I circled around, then came through the back of the café, past the toilets. I finally caught sight of Flynn out the front. He was leaning against one of the tables, watching a couple of tall, slim girls walk past. He turned his head, following them all the way round to the empty concrete paddling pool which stood in the centre of the café foreground.

Then he looked up and saw me. He smiled, but I couldn't smile back. My confidence was dribbling out of my shoes. No way could I compete with girls like that.

He strode over, his face all concerned.

'Hey,' he said uncertainly. 'Are you all right?'

I nodded. I knew I should say something witty and light. But I couldn't. It was just hitting me how mad I was being. Flynn was extraordinary. He was a brilliant actor. He was charismatic. He was good-looking. No way was I even in his league. I might as well go home now.

'River?' Flynn sounded really concerned now. 'What is it?'

I looked up, into his beautiful eyes. He was concentrating on me so hard, it was like the rest of the world didn't exist. It didn't for me, anyway.

'I'm fine,' I said.

But Flynn was staring at me, pulling the truth out of me with his eyes.

He frowned. 'No, you're not. What is it?'

I decided to act all confident and sassy. Bluff it out.

'I'm fine,' I repeated, arching my eyebrows in a way that I hoped was both knowing and attractive. 'I was just wondering why it is that guys always look at hot girls.'

I forced a light laugh, to imply this was an idle thought – of no real importance.

Flynn stared at me. He said nothing, just raised his eyebrows.

'You *know*,' I went on. 'It's that way they can't help but look, if a girl's attractive. Like . . . like there's something programmed into their heads or something.'

'Not their heads.' Flynn grinned. He was still staring at me. Reading me. 'Why don't you think you're hot?' he said slowly.

He'd seen right through me. Right to the heart of what I was thinking. I couldn't believe it. My heart pounded.

'What are you talking about?' I said airily.

Flynn reached out for my wrist and held it lightly in his hand. 'What on earth do you think is wrong with the way you look?' he said, frowning.

I couldn't believe he was asking me. I couldn't believe we'd got into a conversation this heavy within seconds of meeting. I shrugged, wishing he'd stop looking at me. But he didn't. He was waiting for my answer.

'Oh, come on,' I said, making a face. 'I'm not exactly built like a supermodel.' I tried to make it sound like I didn't really care. But I knew I wasn't fooling him.

I stared at the concrete floor.

'River. Listen to me,' Flynn said. 'You look amazing.'

My face was burning. My heart pounding. Did he mean that?

'Okay, so tall, skinny girls look good in designer clothes,' Flynn went on. 'But not everyone wants to go out with a greyhound. Some of us like . . . er . . . er . . .' He paused, frowning.

'Smaller dogs?' I met his eyes properly.

We both laughed. And suddenly all the awkwardness that I'd felt dissolved. Flynn moved closer to me. He put his hand on my waist, then slid it down so that it rested on the curve of my hip. 'Don't you get it? There are bodies that look good. And bodies that feel good. And then there're a few bodies that are both.'

The tips of his fingers were just touching my bum. He lowered his eyes. I could feel them burning through to my breasts and my waist and then down, down through my whole body.

I was so turned on I thought I might faint. How could I feel this connected to someone I hardly knew? My heart pounded. I had no idea what I was doing. What I was supposed to do.

A child cried out right next to us. I suddenly remembered that we were standing just outside the café door, surrounded by other people.

111

Flynn pressed his fingertips against my bum then let go. He smiled. 'Let's go for a walk.'

He took my hand and led me out of the café area and across the open grass. We strolled towards the narrower pathways, whose sides were high with trees and bushes. My head was spinning. My heart racing. I wanted him more than I'd ever wanted anything in my life.

Flynn didn't speak as we crossed the grass, then he stopped and turned to me.

'So, d'you want to find somewhere to sit down?'

I nodded.

We turned down a narrow, secluded path. After a couple of metres Flynn stepped off the path and ducked under a tree, tugging me gently after him. We emerged into a little space hidden between trees and bushes and sat down. The ground was mostly earth, covered with twigs and bits of leaves.

Flynn's eyes gleamed, pale green, in the shadow of the trees and bushes. He moved forward, his fringe falling over his eyes, and kissed my mouth. It was different from the kiss in the classroom. Deeper and sexier. His tongue flickered round mine. Reading me. Just like his eyes had read me earlier.

I wasn't massively experienced, but this was, by miles, the best kiss I'd ever had.

In a whole different kissing league, in fact.

His hand ran down my side, along my back. I put my arms round him and he pulled me closer.

I gasped as his hands moved over me. I heard myself groan – like the noise was coming from far away. His hands were everywhere now, like they were trying to hold all of me at once. Running up my front, and down my back and under my top and across my stomach, and my top half pushed up and I was clawing at him too, pulling him towards me, and he was breathing hard and then his hands moved down . . . over my jeans . . . fumbling for the zip . . .

No.

It was like someone had thrown a bucket of cold water over me. This was too much. Too fast.

'Stop,' I said.

For a split second he froze, then he whipped his hands off me.

I wriggled away. He sat back.

I turned away, my fingers now trembling as I straightened my top. I couldn't believe I'd got so carried away. Now we'd stopped I could hear people on the path just a couple of metres away. I brushed at the back of my head, dusting earth and twigs out of my hair.

'I'm sorry.' He knelt in front of me, his eyes all guarded. 'I don't know what to say . . . I'm sorry . . .'

'It's okay.' I bit my lip. *God*, Emmi had been right. He had gone after sex on the first date. But then so had I. I'd been so gone – so out of my head . . .

'That was scary.' The words came out without me meaning to say them. I hunched over my knees, feeling humiliated. I didn't want him to know how intensely I'd felt just then – how much I'd wanted him. Suddenly I felt raw, like he'd peeled my skin away. I covered my face with my hands. I didn't want to feel such powerful things.

Then I felt his hand on my shoulder.

'River?' His voice was shaky.

I looked up. There were tears in his eyes. I swear to God. Real tears.

'I didn't hurt you, did I?'

I shook my head, this massive lump in my throat. 'No. I just . . . I . . .' I forced a smile. 'I bet Romeo and Juliet didn't have this trouble.'

Flynn smiled back. 'Too busy talking.'

'Maybe we should try that,' I said.

Flynn gazed at me for a long moment. Then he sighed.

'I hate being in that freaking play,' he said.

114

13

I stared at him, genuinely shocked. 'But the play's brilliant and so are you. You say the lines like you really mean them.'

He shrugged. 'I don't mean I hate the play, though I do think a lot of it's stupid. I mean I hate being *in* it. Having to go to rehearsals and staying after school and all that.'

I frowned. 'So why d'you agree to do it, then?'

Flynn glanced sideways at me. 'Promise you won't tell anyone?'

I nodded, a little thrill shooting through me at the idea we had a Secret.

'Nichols begged me to play Romeo. I don't mean he got down on his knees, but he went on and on about it. I kept saying I wasn't interested. In the end he virtually said that if I wanted a good mark on my A level English coursework, I'd better do it.'

I clapped my hand over my mouth. 'You're kidding,' I said.

Flynn stood up. 'So then I turned the tables, didn't I? I said, okay, I'll do the play – though I can't come to rehearsals if I'm working – but only on condition you make *sure* I get a good grade for my coursework.'

My eyes widened. 'No *way*.'

I scrambled to my feet and followed Flynn past the bushes and under the tree. We emerged onto the path together.

'Well, maybe it wasn't quite that blatant.' Flynn casually brushed the earth and stuff off the back of my shirt. 'But we both knew what we were saying. Nichols needs me to be in the play so it isn't a complete frigging shambles. I need to get an A* in my English A level. Sorted.'

I looked up at him, my mind reeling. Now I understood why Mr Nichols always seemed so wary around Flynn – and why he never made a fuss about Flynn missing rehearsals. It was hard to accept – a student and a teacher making that kind of deal. Still, knowing Flynn's personality – and his acting ability – it made total sense.

'I guess you don't need me to tell you how good you are, then,' I said sarcastically.

He put his arm round my shoulders. 'I like you saying it, though,' he said, kissing my hair.

116

We walked on a bit further. I marvelled at how easy it was to be with him. How natural it felt that, even after all that passion, we should just be walking along this path together.

'Why *are* you good at it – acting and stuff?' I said.

Flynn shrugged. 'I've got a good memory, that's all. Nichols explains what the lines mean to me once and I remember. After that, all you have to do is say them naturally.'

Saying them naturally was the hardest part, as far as I was concerned. But the last thing I wanted to do was tell Flynn how brilliant he was again. 'Why d'you say a lot of the play's stupid?' I said. 'I love it, especially all the bits about Romeo and Juliet saying how they feel about each other.'

Flynn laughed. 'There's just so much talking. I mean, you've got to feel sorry for Romeo. He has to go on and on about how fabulous Juliet is, when all he wants to do is have sex with her. I mean, that's what he'd do, if he could. Forget all the poetry. Well, most of it.'

An ice-cold chill settled round my heart. 'Don't you like poetry?' My voice sounded small and vulnerable.

Flynn squeezed my shoulder. 'If you had to choose, between someone you liked writing you poems or kissing you, which would you go for? You can only have one. Forever. Poems or kisses.'

I thought about it. 'Kisses,' I said. 'Because the person would be more there, in the kisses. And so would I. But that doesn't mean I wouldn't like the occasional poem as well.'

He grinned. 'Exactly,' he said.

We wandered back onto the open green and sat down on the grass. The earlier sunshine had faded now behind a thin layer of cloud. I pulled my jacket out of my bag and started putting it on.

'I can't believe you think you're rubbish-looking,' Flynn said, watching me. 'When I saw you in the High Street that time, wearing that top.' He rolled his eyes. 'I wanted to kiss you the whole time we were having that coffee.'

'Did you?' I said, a warm glow spreading right through me.

He reached over and pulled me closer, so our foreheads and noses were almost touching. 'You know what you said, earlier?' His voice was low. 'I don't want to spoil it, okay? We can take it as slow as you want.'

I stared into his eyes, my heart pounding. This was all some mad dream, wasn't it? He was looking at me like . . . like he really wanted me. The whole of me. Not just sex, like Emmi had said. Not cynical, like Mum had warned. But real.

Flynn kissed me lightly, then sat back. 'Can I ask you something?' he said.

I swallowed. 'Sure.'

'How come you've got such a . . . such an . . . *exotic* name?' He chose the word 'exotic' carefully. I loved that. More than anything, I loved that.

That he bothered to find the right word. That he *knew* the right word. That he knew it would matter to me.

'My mum and dad went through this hippy phase,' I said. 'Well, my dad's still in it. They're divorced. Dad lives on this commune in the country – an hour or so outside of London. He probably grows half the vegetables your shop delivers.'

Flynn screwed up his face. 'Don't you mind him dropping out like that?'

I shook my head. 'It's where he belongs. And it's not dropping out, not really. He works as a teacher. Part time. He's just not that bothered about material things. About money.'

I bit my lip, wishing I hadn't mentioned the 'm' word.

'So what about *your* name,' I went on quickly. 'Not Flynn. Your first name. James said it was Patrick. Why don't you let people call you that?'

Flynn lay back on the grass and looked up at the sky. He was silent for so long I thought he wasn't going to answer me. When he did speak his voice had an edge to it.

'Patrick's my dad's name,' he said.

I frowned, not understanding. Okay, so he didn't get on with his dad . . . but . . .

'But isn't Flynn your dad's name as well?'

He shook his head, not looking at me. 'They never got married.'

'I see,' I said, not really seeing at all. 'So what do your sisters call you? Surely they can't call you Flynn if it's their surname too?'

Flynn rolled over onto his side. 'What's the time?'

I checked my phone. 'Almost five.'

He got up. 'I gotta go,' he said. 'I've got to pick Caitlin up from a friend's near home, then come back for Siobhan at six. And I'm doing an extra shift at the café tonight.'

'Jeez, Flynn,' I said, scrambling to my feet beside him. 'Anyone would think you were responsible for your entire family.' I meant it as a joke, but Flynn stared at me with this icy look in his eye.

'I am,' he said. 'My mum works two jobs. She can't be at home all the time. I have to look after the others.'

I blinked at him, this panicky feeling rising in my chest. I didn't want us to part like this – him all cross.

Not after how brilliant it had been earlier, when he'd said all that about taking things slow.

We stared at each other for a moment, then he slid his arms round my waist. *God*, he felt good – his back all solid and muscular. I sank against his chest. I could feel his heart beating under the thin cotton top he was wearing.

'I wasn't laughing at you,' I said quietly. 'I think it's amazing how responsible you are. Most guys your age only think about themselves.'

He bent down to find my face. He kissed my nose, then my mouth.

We stood there for I don't know how long, just lost in that kiss.

And then he pulled away. 'Sorry I snapped at you before,' he said quietly. 'I just feel guilty sometimes.'

I wanted to ask him what he meant. Guilty about *what*, for goodness' sake? But he was brushing the grass off his jumper, already walking towards the park exit. I strolled beside him, my heart in my mouth.

When am I going to see you again?

Despite all my earlier directness I couldn't quite bring myself to ask it. He didn't say anything until we got to the park gates and turned towards the High Street.

'So, d'you want to meet up tomorrow?' he said.

'I've got loads of essays and stuff to do, but I could see you in the afternoon. Mum and Siob'll be at work and Caitlin's doing some half-term school club thing.'

I gazed up at his earnest face, suddenly seeing how much he wanted me to want to see him again.

'Sure,' I smiled. 'I'd love to.'

14

I Facebooked Emmi and Grace, then, later, we went out. We ended up in this little pasta restaurant, eating spaghetti in tomato sauce and talking about boys.

I told them it had been good with Flynn, but that I was being sensible, emotionally. . . seeing how things went . . . It was a total lie, of course, but I couldn't tell them the truth. It was somehow too precious, too private.

Anyway, Emmi did enough talking for the three of us. She and Alex were spending most of their time together now – and as far as Grace and I could work out, all they did was have sex. Emmi delighted in telling us all the different places they'd done it.

'At the swimming baths on Friday afternoon. We were both soaking wet in this changing cubicle . . .'

Grace frowned. 'Weren't you cold?'

Emmi ignored her. 'Then that night, going home,

on the top deck of the number 91. That was awesome. There were these guys at the front of the bus, they didn't have a clue.' Emmi twirled up a forkful of spaghetti. She lowered her voice. 'Then this afternoon,' she said, 'we went to the cinema. Really boring film. So we crept out and did it in the ladies' toilets.'

She shoved the spaghetti into her mouth and smiled triumphantly at us.

I stared at her. How could she be so matter-of-fact about it? She made it sound like a list of places she'd cleaned her teeth.

Not for the first time, I felt completely confused over Emmi's unemotional attitude to sex. I'd never gone all the way myself, of course, but I could imagine with Flynn it would be mind-blowing. A massive deal.

Grace wrinkled up her snubby little nose. 'Eew, Emmi, the ladies' . . . ? You could have caught something,' she said.

'No, I couldn't. We used a condom,' Emmi said defiantly.

'She means from the toilet.' I grinned, then shook my head solemnly. 'You're a class act, Em. A class act.'

But Emmi didn't seem to mind us teasing her. In fact, the more we made it clear we weren't impressed, the more she looked down her nose at us both – as if there was something wrong with us for not having lost our virginity yet. As if we lacked something important – originality maybe, or confidence or nerve.

No. There was no way I could tell them how it had felt with Flynn in the park. How scarily powerful my feelings had been. How I'd felt when he'd kissed and touched me – like my heart was full to bursting and my breath was being sucked out of me and my head was exploding with it.

Flynn and I met up as arranged the next day. It was warm again and we sat out on the open grass in the park. Flynn was working on some history essay. I'd brought a book, but I didn't read much. I just sat there, leaning against Flynn's legs, enjoying the sun on my face.

I still couldn't believe how easy it was just to be with him. It was like we'd known each other for ages. Like we didn't need to speak at all.

Flynn worked fast, his lips moving silently as he read from his textbooks then wrote another few sentences. After ten minutes or so he seemed to be concentrating so hard I wasn't sure he was even aware of my presence.

I turned back to my book, but I couldn't follow

the words on the page. Every thought in my head, every sense in my body was tuned to him. I knew there was so much he kept secret, hidden away from everyone. I was greedy for more of him.

I closed my book and turned round, gazing at his face.

He looked up straight away. 'Sorry, I won't be much longer.' He stared down at the essay. 'I've got to finish this today. I said I'd go and help Mum with her work tomorrow and then I'm doing some extra shifts at Goldbar's on Wednesday and Thursday.'

I took a deep breath. I knew that talking about Flynn's jobs was dangerous territory. It was too close to talking about him not having any money.

'What work does your mum do?' I said tentatively.

Flynn met my gaze. His eyes darkened, as if daring me to take the mickey. 'Cleaning jobs,' he said shortly. 'And she does shifts at this call centre in Archway too.'

I nodded slowly, sensing that if I said the wrong thing now, he might get up and stalk off.

'Please don't get cross,' I said. 'But why did you say the other day that you feel guilty about your mum and sister working?' I took his hand.

His eyes glittered dangerously. But he didn't pull his hand away.

'Because they're bringing in more money than me,' he muttered.

I frowned. 'But you're at school, and you work all the time when you're not.'

'Exactly,' he said. 'I'm still at school. I could have left last year. I could be working full time, really helping. Instead, they're having to pay for me. Well, Mum's money plus benefits pays the rent and bills. And Siobhan pays for food. My money just means we can buy new clothes occasionally. I hate it.'

His eyes burned so fiercely that I felt scared and turned on all at once.

'So why did you stay on?'

'I need A levels to get to law school,' he said. 'Once I'm a lawyer I'll earn ten times more money than you get from doing rubbish cleaning jobs and car washing and stupid organic vegetable deliveries.'

'You want to be a lawyer?' I screwed up my face. It was hard to imagine Flynn sitting in some office, wearing a suit, poring over boring law books.

'No.' Flynn sighed. He let go of my hand and picked at a blade of grass on the ground between us. 'Not really. But I want a profession . . . something that people have heard of. Something that'll make people respect me. And I want to earn a lot of money. So I can look after my mum.' His voice was very low.

He sounded cross, but I was pretty sure he was just embarrassed again.

'What about your dad?' I asked timidly. 'Doesn't he help with money?'

Flynn snorted with derision. I waited a second, hoping he'd say more, but he didn't. I wanted to push him, but his face looked so thunderous I didn't dare. I decided to get back to the earlier part of the conversation.

'Why d'you want to be a lawyer?' I said. 'Why not a doctor? Or . . . or an accountant?'

I wanted him to say something noble – about wanting to fight for people's rights or keep criminals off the streets or something.

Instead, he just sighed. 'Well, I can do maths, but I don't really like it. And science is boring – at least the GCSE courses were,' he said. 'A lawyer's just easier. And there's lots of money in the commercial stuff.'

I sat there, trying to get my head around this – I had never thought about work like that. I had thoughts sometimes of being a journalist or a therapist, maybe. And I suppose I had an idea that they would both be quite well paid. But I couldn't imagine picking a career solely on how much money I could make from it.

'How many people know?' I said.

He glanced up at me. 'That I want to be a lawyer?'

I shook my head. '*Why* you want to be a lawyer?'

'Just Mum and Siob.' His eyes bored into me. 'And you.' He looked down at the blade of grass he'd picked up, then split it with his thumbnail. 'I don't know why, but I seem to keep telling you things.'

I took a moment to savour this – to let it flow through me, warming me – then I asked him about his previous girlfriends.

Flynn shrugged a bit, then admitted to a few meaningless (he said) one-nighters, and two girls he'd gone out with for a couple of months each. He said he couldn't even remember their names.

I guess it wasn't really that much, but compared to my track record it felt like a lot of experience. I'd done plenty of disappointing kissing over the past two years, but I'd only really had one proper boyfriend before. Oliver Brown. I'd met him at a party last year and talked to him because he had nice eyes. We'd gone out for three months, but all we'd done was kiss and fumble about a bit. I dumped him in the end because I knew I didn't love him and liking and fancying him a little just wasn't enough.

Flynn and I met up for a few snatched hours most days that half-term. We talked more – about school and the subjects Flynn had chosen for his AS and A levels. He was doing history, English, French and geography. As I was planning to do the first two of those next year, I asked him lots of questions about what books he had to read and what he thought of them. I soon realised Flynn viewed books completely differently from me. I loved getting lost in the stories, the world of the characters. For him, they were simply a means to an end – a means to a qualification that he hoped would bring him status and money. I don't mean he didn't ever enjoy reading. But he never seemed to care about stories like I did.

I learned to avoid mentioning the things that made him angry. It was quite a list. In addition to drunks and money, he had already snapped at me when I'd asked about him being Catholic:

'I'm not Catholic. Not any more. It's hypocritical and hard-faced and totally up its own arse. I got out of it as soon as I could. Okay?'

He got angriest of all when I asked him questions about his home and his family, especially why he was so protective of Siobhan. Once or twice he shouted at me. I learned to stop speaking as soon as his face got that thundery, closed-down look that meant he was on the verge of losing his temper.

I told myself it didn't really matter.

We still had plenty to talk about. I told him loads about my mum and dad and how it had been when they split up. I talked about Stone – how he called me Swampy and how annoying he was. I talked about the books I'd read and the films I'd seen and the things I'd done with my friends.

Flynn told me about his jobs. Goldbar's where he worked on Sundays was a gym. Well, a boxing club, really. He got free classes and some money in exchange for cleaning the place.

'I like boxing,' he said, when I asked him why he did it. 'It's important. So I can look after myself.'

'You mean fight?' I said. 'Why d'you need to be able to do that?'

He muttered something vague about rough neighbourhoods.

But I knew there was something else too.

Something he wouldn't say.

What we talked about most, of course, was *Romeo and Juliet* – how good or bad various people were in their parts. How much Mr Nichols irritated him. How boring we both found bits of the play – and how brilliant some of it was.

One day I questioned him carefully about Emmi and what it was like acting with her.

'It's okay.' He shrugged. 'I mean, she's all right as Juliet, but she's a bit . . .' He paused, flicking an imaginary strand of hair off his shoulder and pouting at me in a wickedly accurate imitation of Emmi.

131

'I dunno, sometimes I think she's more concerned about looking good than anything else.'

I grinned, then felt disloyal.

'Emmi's okay,' I protested. 'I know she comes across as a bit superficial, but she's a good friend.'

Flynn nodded.

'And she *does* look good,' I said. 'She's really pretty.'

'Well, that's true,' Flynn acknowledged.

There was a short pause. A thin thread of jealousy twisted into a knot in my heart. Flynn thought Emmi was really pretty.

Well, of course he did. Who wouldn't?

It didn't mean he liked her more than me.

Flynn put his arms round me. 'Never mind Emmi. Doing *Romeo and Juliet*'s not real. It's not like with you.'

And he drew me into this long kiss. Our kisses were – unbelievably – getting better and better. He didn't try to touch me that much, not inside my jeans, anyway, not the whole time we were meeting in the park. But he still ran his hands all over me as we kissed. I shivered wherever he touched me.

He laughed at that, told me how sexy I was.

But it wasn't me who was sexy.

It was him.

It was us. Together.

15

Half-term slid slowly by. By the last weekend the weather had changed completely. After the mild, still days of earlier in the week, the temperature dropped and it started raining – not hard, but off and on, all the time.

It was too cold and wet to sit outdoors in the park. Especially for Flynn – who either didn't have a coat or only possessed one he was ashamed to be seen in. I hadn't plucked up the courage to ask which yet.

On Friday I forced him to let me buy him a coffee at the café we'd gone to that very first time. He agreed – after all it was only fair, even he could see that, as he'd bought the last one. But just talking about money seemed to put him in a bad mood. I knew he was embarrassed that I had more than him. I suppose I still didn't really understand why it was such a big deal – after all, it wasn't like I was rich or anything.

I kept waiting for him to ask me round to his house. But he didn't. So in the end we agreed to meet on Sunday afternoon at mine. I would rather we'd gone to a cheap café, but I was too scared of us having an argument over who was going to pay.

I hadn't told Mum very much about Flynn – just that we'd met up a couple of times and that he was coming round so we could test each other on our lines. This, of course, wasn't even remotely true – Flynn had been word-perfect from the first rehearsal, while I knew half the entire play off by heart.

Stone was staying over at Dad's all weekend and I knew Mum would be out until about five. Flynn said he'd come round at four. It was all going to work, I told myself nervously. He'd have an hour to get used to the place before having to meet Mum. She'd teased me no end when I told her Flynn was playing Romeo.

'So you still want to be Juliet, then?' she'd said, nudging me like she'd said something hilarious.

I'd looked forward to him coming round all day, but as soon as I opened the door and saw him standing outside, I knew it was going to be a disaster.

His arms were crossed and his face was all clenched up. I could practically feel the anger pulsing off him as I took him through the hall into the kitchen. We had a can of Coke and some biscuits.

Flynn said nothing. I chattered away about seeing Emmi and Grace the night before. I just wanted to keep the conversation light and easy. But I guess it was hard for Flynn to hear how we'd all gone out to the pub while he'd been working. How Emmi and Grace had spent the evening with Alex and James. How all these other boys had been there too.

I stressed I'd only had one drink, then I tried to say something about missing him, about nobody last night being half as interesting as he was, but he cut me off.

'Can I see your room then?' he said aggressively.

I took him upstairs feeling deeply uneasy.

I'd spent ages tidying my room, then messing it up a bit so it didn't look too neat and ordered. But Flynn didn't take much notice – he glanced round at the wooden wardrobe and the little desk and the blue-and-green check duvet and the table covered with pots and bottles. Then he strode over to the window and stared outside. I walked up behind him. He was gripping his drink so tightly that his knuckles were white.

'Flynn?' I said. 'What's wrong?'

He turned round, this vicious look in his eye. 'You're never going to understand, are you?'

'Understand what?' My heart pounded.

'What you have.' He waved his arm around, as if to indicate the whole house. 'All this. All this amazing wealth. You take it all for granted, don't you?'

'No.' I frowned. 'And we're not wealthy. My mum works. And my dad gives us what he can. Okay, so there's enough money for this house, but we're not rich or anything. I don't see—'

'No,' Flynn snapped. 'You don't see at all. You don't see what it's like when you don't have anything.' His voice got deeper and louder, like it was catching in his throat. 'You don't see what it's like when you worry about money all the time. When you work and work and it all goes on rent and crap food and crap clothes and there's nothing left over even for a pair of frigging shoes.' He spat the last few words out at me, his whole face darkened with anger.

A sick, angry knot lodged itself in my chest.

'It's not my fault,' I said, trying to stop my voice from shaking. 'I didn't make it like this.' Tears welled up in my eyes and I turned away, not wanting him to see how much he'd upset me.

'I realised something the other day doing that stupid play,' Flynn snarled. 'There's this line of Romeo's:

"Need and oppression starveth in thy eyes,
Contempt and beggary hangs upon thy back . . ."

'You know how I know how to say that? It's because I've lived it.' His voice rose. 'I've seen the need in my mum's eyes. How she's weighed down by people's contempt for her because she's got no money.' He was shouting now. 'People like you make me—'

'Stop it!' I yelled, turning to face him. 'Okay, so you've got no money. That doesn't give you the right to hate everyone who has a little bit more. D'you hear me, Flynn? It's not my family's fault that you're not well off. We don't look down on you or your mum. That's in your head.'

The kitchen door slammed downstairs. Mum's ever so subtle way of letting me know she was back. *Great.* I wondered how much of our shouting match she'd heard.

Flynn was gazing down at me, this unreadable expression in his eyes. I put my hands on his arms. Immediately, I could feel the tension leaking out of them, his shoulders releasing down.

'I'm sorry,' he mumbled awkwardly. 'I just hate it that I can't go out with you properly. That you get to go out on a Saturday night with loads of blokes sniffing around. That you probably spend more money in one hour than I make all day.'

He let out a long, heavy sigh.

I twisted my arms up round his neck. His eyes were so beautiful – all soulful in the dimming light. 'Actually, I hardly spent any money last night.' I grinned. 'Boys kept buying me drinks.'

Flynn stared at me.

'Is that supposed to make me feel better?' he grunted. But a small smile started to creep across his mouth. He looked into my eyes, this deep, sexy look. 'So you didn't buy any drinks back?' He smoothed his hands over my waist.

I shivered, then stood on tiptoe, reaching up for him. 'No, I saved all my money so I could buy *you* a drink tonight.' I kissed him quickly before he could say anything, then drew back. 'Please let me, Flynn. Please don't make this a big deal. Why can't you see it's only money – and if I happen to have a few quid more than you, why can't we just share it?'

He looked down at me, his eyes like golden flints. 'It doesn't work that way,' he said.

'But it could,' I smiled. 'We can make it work however we want. It's not like you'd be sponging off me. I mean, you earn loads of money. Well, some, anyway. And you give all that to your mum, don't you?'

He nodded.

'So all I'm doing is giving some of it back to you.'

'That's the most ridiculous thing I've ever heard,' he laughed, kissing me gently. Then he nuzzled at my ear. 'You're a bold piece,' he murmured, running his hands down my bum. 'A—'

Without warning, Mum opened the door.

Flynn and I both jumped. I sprang back, away from him.

Mum looked Flynn up and down, then she turned to me. I could feel my face burning.

'Finished learning your lines, then?' she said, her voice heavy with sarcasm.

'Why didn't you knock?' I snapped.

Mum ignored me. She turned to Flynn expectantly.

He said nothing.

Mum strode across my bedroom carpet, her arm outstretched. 'I'm assuming you're Flynn?'

He shook her hand. I noticed, with some admiration, that he did so without either blushing or flinching.

And Mum looked pretty terrifying. She was wearing an expensive-looking suit and loads of make-up. In her heels she was nearly as tall as Flynn.

She stood back, still staring at him. 'I heard shouting,' she said.

Oh God.

'It was just the play, Mum,' I said quickly. 'We were going over our lines.'

Mum raised an eyebrow. 'I don't remember a scene in *Romeo and Juliet* where Romeo starts shouting at the Nurse?'

Flynn folded his arms. His face took on the same sullen expression I'd seen him give Mr Nichols a thousand times.

'It wasn't the play,' he said. 'River and I were arguing.'

'Oh?' Mum raised her eyebrows. 'What about?'

'*Mu-um*.' My heart was in my mouth. The tension between Mum and Flynn was practically touchable.

Flynn stared at her stonily.

'Well?' Mum drew herself up. 'I think I have a right to know why you were shouting at my daughter in my own house.'

'Actually you don't,' Flynn said, now looking bored. 'It's none of your business.'

'Flynn.' I gaped at him. Okay, so Mum was being impossible, but couldn't he hear how rude he sounded?

Mum blinked. 'I'd like you to leave, Flynn,' she said.

What? No. How was this happening?

'Wait,' I said.

140

But Flynn was already walking to the door. 'Bye, River,' he said without looking round.

I heard his feet on the stairs. I ran to the door.

'River,' Mum snapped. 'You're not going after him.'

I spun round. 'Why did you have to be like that?' I shouted. Then I turned and ran downstairs.

Flynn was almost at the end of the road when I caught up with him. I grabbed his hand and we walked along in silence for a minute. I didn't know where I was going. Just that I couldn't bear to leave him with all that anger still swirling around between us.

I kept thinking about the way he had glared at Mum. Why had he done that? Why had he not at least tried to be nice?

Flynn glanced down at me. 'Well, that went well,' he grinned.

'Flynn, it's not funny,' I said. 'Why did you have to wind her up like that?'

He made a face. 'She was rude to me first,' he said.

I rolled my eyes, 'Can you hear how childish you sound?' I said.

Flynn shook my hand out of his. He stopped walking and looked at me, his face all thundery and closed up. 'Fine. Run back to Mummy, then.'

I exploded.

'Jeez, Flynn. Going out with you is like being with a frigging bomb.'

I stopped. I hadn't meant to say 'going out'. The truth was that although we'd spent a huge amount of time together this week, neither of us had talked about whether we were official or not.

Flynn frowned at me. 'What?'

'You know,' I went on, ignoring the 'going out' part of what I'd said. 'Say the wrong thing and you're liable to blow up. No warning. No prisoners. No grey areas. Just a big Pow.'

Flynn's eyes lightened into the shadow of a smile. 'A big *Pow*?' he said slowly.

I stared at him, my anger draining away. I couldn't stay mad. He was just too . . . too *right*. I loved everything about his face – the way the nose sloped and the lips curled. It was the most subtle, expressive face I'd ever seen in my life.

I shivered. I'd run out of the house in just a T-shirt, and it was getting dark outside and the air was cold. Flynn put his hands on my arms, just like he had that night when I'd been sick. His face relaxed into a beautiful grin.

'So we are officially going out, then?' he said, pulling me towards him.

My breath caught in my throat.

'I guess,' I grunted, sliding my arms round his

back, wanting him so badly I could die. 'So long as you can keep your big Pows under control.'

I shivered again. He rubbed my back. 'If I had a jacket, I'd let you wear it, you know,' he murmured.

'Yeah.' I mimicked the harsh, deep way he'd spoken earlier. 'But you're too poor to have a frigging jacket.'

For a second I wondered if he'd get all offended again, but he didn't.

'Actually I do have a jacket,' he laughed, 'but it's so hideous I can't bring myself to wear it. My mum bought it when I wasn't there. Two pounds in some second-hand shop. A frigging fortune for her. She was so pleased with herself. But it's horrible. Like something my da would . . .' He stopped, suddenly, and buried his face in my hair. 'Hey, River,' he said – and his voice sounded muffled. 'D'you still want to go for a drink?'

I nodded.

He started kissing my neck, holding me tight. I held my breath, knowing something between us had shifted. That we were closer, somehow. That he was starting to let me in.

'I reckon I've got enough money to buy you one drink,' he murmured. 'And I can drink tap water. Then you can buy me an orange juice. Then I'll just carry on drinking water.'

'Hey, Flynn.' I gently pushed his face away from me. The look in his eyes was achingly tender. I wanted to tell him that I was falling in love with him. But it wasn't the right time.

Not now. Not yet. Not quite.

16

Three weeks passed. Flynn and I met up as often as we could. After rehearsals and at the weekends. Most of the time we were on our own, though sometimes we hung out with Grace and James.

Flynn never joined in the rounds of drinks that were bought. He occasionally let me or James buy him an orange juice – but he was always careful to buy drinks back for us afterwards.

I lost count of the number of times I watched him, hunched and brooding, counting out his coins in the palm of his hand before he went to the bar or agonising over whether he could afford a packet of crisps or a last cup of coffee.

I'd never spent time with somebody who watched every single penny like that. I mean, don't get me wrong – none of us were loaded. Except Emmi, of course. Everyone else had to be really careful about what they spent. But with Flynn it went deeper. Like he was wrestling with his conscience every time he bought something. As more time went by, I began to understand why he hated not having money so much.

It dominated his whole life. Everything he did. Everything he planned to do in the future.

We talked more about his ambition to become a lawyer. I felt deeply uncomfortable that he didn't seem to be in the slightest bit interested in law. Just in the money he would be able to make. The respect he would be able to buy.

It kind of went against everything I'd been brought up with. I tried to say this to Flynn, but he got angry, accusing me of not understanding him. Again.

I half wanted to talk to Dad about it, but I hadn't seen him since the potato-digging day. I'd refused to go up to the commune the last few weeks. Stone and I usually went on Sundays – but now Sundays were the days I spent time with Flynn.

Mum hated me seeing him. When I got home that first Sunday, hours after she'd thrown him out of the house, we'd had a long talk about our relationship – Flynn's and mine. She kept going on about how intense he'd seemed, how angry.

'I've seen boys like that before,' she said. 'Pushing against authority all the time. He's trouble, River.'

'God, Mum, stop being such a Nazi,' I snarled at

her. But I knew she was partly right. Flynn did push against authority all the time. He was always slagging off the adults where he worked. And how often had I seen him be breathtakingly rude to Mr Nichols?

I half expected Mum to forbid me to see Flynn. But I think she knew coming down hard on us would only make me more determined to be with him. So she kept quiet, hoping we'd lose interest in each other, and contented herself with quoting teenage pregnancy statistics at me and muttering dark warnings about Not Getting Carried Away.

Flynn refused to come round to the house again. I could tell Mum was relieved about that. To be honest, I think Flynn scared her a little. I think he scared most people. The scruffy school uniform he wore, the brilliant way he acted in the play, his lack of money and, above all, his whole not-drinking thing – all of these things set him apart. But, despite being different, he wasn't ridiculed or ignored like most people would have been.

Instead, he was admired and feared. Not liked particularly. I had to admit it. He was too much of a loner for that. And I could see that though most people thought he could sometimes be a laugh, only James actually considered him a friend. I liked seeing them together – there was something about James's bumbling, kindly manner that seemed to rub away Flynn's hard edges. They spent a lot of time discussing boxing and football – neither of which I was remotely interested in.

I occasionally saw Flynn's older sister, Siobhan, when I went with him to pick her up from her hairdressing job. What I'd initially taken to be hostility turned out to be crippling shyness. Siobhan often threw me a quick, nervous smile – but she hardly spoke when I was around and never looked me properly in the eye.

I wondered if her chronic shyness had something to do with why Flynn was so protective of her, but I'd long stopped attempting to ask him about that.

It was the middle of November. Rehearsals for *Romeo and Juliet* were both more fun and more hard work than they had been before. We were using the proper stage now, at the back of the school's large assembly hall. Mr Nichols had appointed Maz – a friend of Alex's – as stage manager. Everyone liked him, but his assistant, Liam, wasn't so popular. Flynn, in particular, hated the way Liam so evidently enjoyed ordering us around, demanding that we signed our props in and out of the little cupboard in the wings.

The art teacher was roped in to supervise both scenery and costumes. Mr Nichols was going for a

148

modern-day setting, so they got hold of plain black suits for Flynn and James and the other main male characters. Emmi was wearing this silky blue evening dress with tiny straps. It was pretty tatty close up, but from a distance, on stage, it looked beautiful.

I had to wear a nanny's uniform – a black top and skirt with a starchy white apron. Flynn said it was sexy. I knew it was entirely hideous.

I'd hardly spoken to Emmi for days. She and Alex were still at it like maniacs – even managing to do it up against the props cupboard one evening while everyone else listened to Mr Nichols' notes. But it didn't stop Emmi from flirting with the other guys at rehearsals and doing that hair-flicking thing Flynn had so brilliantly mimicked.

I felt anxious whenever I thought about her and Flynn kissing in the play. But it hadn't happened yet and I tried not to dwell on it.

Then one week at the end of November, when the performances were only two weeks away, she insisted Flynn and I come out after rehearsal with her and Alex. I didn't really want to go, but Emmi can be pretty persuasive. She made a big show of wanting to buy everyone drinks – and I convinced Flynn it would be all right and that she would definitely not be expecting either of us to buy any back. So the four of us – plus Grace and James – set off for this local pub that turns a blind eye to dodgy ID.

The guys went up to the bar with Emmi's money and bought us all drinks. Emmi had asked for a revolting-looking bright pink alcopop with an extra shot of vodka. She knocked it back in about two minutes, and then told Alex to get her some more.

I could see he wasn't pleased about this, but he did it.

Ten minutes later Emmi was on her fourth round and starting to lose her few remaining inhibitions.

'Hey, Flynn,' she slurred. 'When d'you think we'll have to kiss? On stage.'

My heart thudded. Next to Emmi, Alex stiffened.

Flynn gazed at Emmi coolly. 'When Mr Nichols tells us to,' he said, his voice dripping with irritation.

Emmi leaned over. 'Yeah.' She grinned drunkenly. 'I'm not looking forward to it either.'

There was a tense pause.

'Emmi.' I stared at her. 'That's enough.'

She sat back, smiling. 'Oh, calm down, River,' she giggled. 'I'm just trying to make everyone feel okay about it. I mean, let's face it, it's going to be awkward enou—'

'No, it's not,' Flynn snapped. 'It's not awkward at all. It's just kissing. A bit of lip contact. Nothing more.'

Emmi jugged back the last of her current drink. 'A bit of lip contact.' She giggled again, then looked over at me. 'I feel sorry for you, River, if that's all kissing means to him.'

I could feel Flynn tensing beside me. I slipped my arm round his waist.

'Ignore her,' I whispered. 'Kiss me.'

He dragged his chair back a little way, pulling me down onto his lap. I reached for his face, smiling. At first his lips were taut on mine – tense with his anger at Emmi, but I slid my tongue between them, trying to tell him how much I wanted him, and he relaxed into the kiss.

At first I held back, feeling self-conscious. *God*, a second ago Emmi had been talking about us kissing and now here we were, doing so in public.

Then the kiss deepened. Flynn slid his hand under my shirt. I still didn't like the idea that other people could see us, but on the other hand, they were all busy talking. And, anyway, Flynn was only running his fingers up and down my back. I could feel my skin break out in goosebumps as he touched me. He brought his hands up to my face, holding me, stroking me. I forgot all the people around us. Everything

151

was about Flynn. I slid my own hands under his shirt, feeling the hard muscles, the firm, square shape of his body.

'OH, DO WHAT YOU WANT!'

The deep male roar jolted me back to the pub. I turned away from Flynn in time to see Alex pushing back his chair and storming away from the table. Emmi, at whom he had evidently been shouting, was sitting – looking mutinous – in front of the remains of yet another drink.

The door of the pub slammed shut. Alex disappeared. I stared at Emmi. Two fat tears trickled down her cheeks. I frowned. Something was very wrong. Emmi never cried.

She stood up and launched herself in the direction of the toilets.

I leaned across to Grace and James. 'What happened?'

Grace frowned. 'Emmi was asking Alex to buy another round and he was saying he thought she'd had enough and she got really mad and then he stormed off.'

I got up and turned to Flynn. 'I'm going to see if she's all right.'

He rolled his eyes but nodded, then turned back to the table. I headed for the toilets with Grace at my side.

We found Emmi in the end cubicle, crying her eyes out.

'What's going on?' I asked, as I stood in the door-way. My hands were shaking. I was afraid she was going to say that she fancied Flynn or something, but she just kept crying and moaning.

'Is it just that you had that row with Alex?' Grace said timidly.

Emmi bawled louder. 'No.'

'Are you pregnant?' I said.

'No.' Emmi stopped crying and stared at us exasperatedly. 'It's nothing to do with a boy.'

She bent over and started weeping again. Grace and I exchanged anxious glances. 'What then?' I said. 'Is it something at home?'

'Oh, for God's sake!' Emmi straightened up, her eyes flashing with impatience. 'It's the play.'

17

There was a stunned silence. What on earth did she mean? My mind went back to Flynn. Was it something to do with acting with him?

I shook her arm. '*What* about the play, Emmi? *What?*'

There was a long silence. Emmi stopped crying. She teetered over to the basins and started splashing water on her face.

Then she stood up. 'I'm scared,' she said. She looked at our reflections in the mirror. 'I'm really scared of how hard it is and how bad I am and how much everyone will laugh when they see me.'

I stared at her in the mirror. She couldn't be serious. Emmi was the most confident person I knew. And, even now, with red, puffy eyes, she still looked beautiful.

Grace shook her head. 'But Emmi, you'll be fine. You know the part and you look great and—'

'I'm not as good as Flynn,' Emmi said. She turned round and stared at me – eye to eye. 'He's brilliant. I can't do it as well as him.' Her lip trembled and she stumbled into my arms.

I held her as she wept. Grace slipped out, mouthing she was going to tell the boys we were going and call a cab.

Emmi was still sobbing. I patted her on the back, like Mum used to with me and Stone when we were sick. I could barely believe what she'd said. Emmi scared? Emmi insecure? Ever since I'd met her on day one at Langton Girls Grammar, Emmi had always been super-confident about everything.

'Thanks, Riv,' Emmi mumbled. 'You're a really good friend, especially after what I said earlier . . .' She sniffed. 'I know I was a cow.'

I felt a surge of affection for her.

'Hey, Em.' I hugged her again. 'That doesn't matter and – by the way – you *can* do Juliet . . . you're good at it. You just have to imagine it. Hard.'

She gulped, nodding. Then she closed her eyes.

'Could we go outside for a minute?' she said. 'Get some air.'

'Sure.' I led her out of the toilets. There was a fire door at the far end of the corridor, propped open with a cardboard box. We slipped through it, into an alleyway at the back of the pub. The air was bitingly

155

cold. I hugged my arms round my chest. Emmi wandered over to the brick wall at the end and sat on it, tipping her head back to the star-filled sky.

'I wish you were playing Juliet, Riv,' she said quietly.

I leaned against the wall beside the fire door, watching my breath send a white mist into the chilly night air. 'Yeah, well I'm not. Mr Nichols picked you.'

'Only because you screwed up that second audition thing we did.' Emmi laughed. 'You were miles better than me first time round. And I bet you only messed it up later because you fancied Flynn. Which is ironic, isn't it? That falling for Romeo stopped you getting the part of Juliet.'

I took a deep gulp of the cold air. I'd never seen it like that before. But it was true. And Emmi was right, it was ironic.

The fire door beside me lurched violently open, almost slamming back into my face. Two blokes – older teenagers, I guessed – staggered out into the alleyway. They were big, thickset guys – one with fair hair, the other dark.

It was too gloomy in the alleyway to make out their faces properly.

The guy with dark hair spotted Emmi instantly. 'Well, hello,' he said in a silly, deep voice. 'We come out for a slash and we find a babe. You looking for company?'

Emmi shook her head and jumped off the wall. Unfortunately, she was still pretty drunk, so she landed unevenly and stumbled sideways. The dark-haired guy was beside her in less than a second.

'Hey, let me help you,' he said.

The fair-haired guy stood behind him as he helped Emmi to her feet, his hands all over her bum.

I watched open-mouthed. I wanted to move – to rescue Emmi, to run inside to get help. But my feet had frozen to the ground. Neither of the two guys had seen me standing next to the fire door.

Emmi tried to pull away. The dark-haired boy grabbed her arm. 'Don't be like that,' he said nastily. 'I was trying to help you.'

He put his hand under her skirt. Emmi started struggling more violently. She backed away across the concrete. My heart pounded.

Do something. Get help.

The dark-haired guy turned to his mate, laughing.

That's when he saw me.

'Look,' he said softly. 'She's even brought a friend.'

The fair-haired, thickset guy strode towards me. He bent low over me, his breath all beery and sour.

His face was in shadow, but I could just make out the sneer on his face.

'Come on.' Beer Breath grabbed my arm. 'We can have a party.'

'No.' I wanted to scream, but my voice had shrunk to a terrified whisper.

I tried to wrench myself away, but he was far, far stronger than me. In seconds he'd dragged me over to where his friend was still trying to grope Emmi. She was sobbing and struggling.

'River,' she wailed. 'Make him stop.'

Panic whirled in my chest. 'Please don't do this,' I said, my voice still tiny. 'We just want to go back inside.'

Beer Breath gripped my arm harder. 'Now that's not very nice.' He looked over at his friend. 'We only want to party a bit, yeah?'

Emmi was hunched over, weeping. The dark-haired guy threw his mate a smug grin and tried to pull Emmi towards him again.

She resisted.

The grin slid off the guy's face. 'Come on, you stupid cow. I saw you earlier – you're off your head, so don't pretend you're not up for it.'

'No,' Emmi whimpered.

As I stared at her terrified, tear-stained face, my own terror turned to fury. I lurched away from Beer Breath, finding my voice at last.

'Get off us,' I screamed. 'GO AWAY!'

He was still holding me tightly. Then someone streaked through the alleyway, so fast I could barely make him out.

Flynn. He hurled himself at Beer Breath. Shoved him hard in the chest.

'Don't touch her,' he spat. Then he punched. *Crunch*. His fist smashed into the guy's nose.

Beer Breath let go of me. Staggered backwards, his hands over his face.

'You . . . you . . .' He let out a stream of swear words as blood spurted from between his fingers. 'You freakin' broke my nose!'

Flynn spun round, fists clenched. But the dark-haired guy was already there. I heard the smack of his fist against Flynn's face. Flynn reeled backwards. I ran round, blood pounding in my ears.

'Get off him,' I yelled. I kicked out, my foot making contact with the guy's leg.

He groaned. Then Flynn was back. He swung his fist up under the guy's chin. *Wham*. The guy stumbled sideways. He clutched at Beer Breath's arm.

'Come on . . .' Beer Breath stumbled away from us, still swearing at Flynn, dragging his friend into the alley.

'Pussies,' Flynn roared. '*Wankers*.'

Suddenly the alleyway was flooded with light as

someone turned on a light inside the pub. I caught a glimpse of Flynn's face, contorted with rage. The two guys disappeared down the alleyway.

I turned round. Emmi was slumped on the ground beside the wall. She was bent over, sobbing. I looked at Flynn.

He was panting, his eyes livid with fury. And then the fury fell away and his eyes filled with concern.

'Are you all right?'

I nodded. I could hear voices just inside the pub. People would be here any second. Flynn turned his head away so I couldn't see his face. But I walked round in front of him.

His mouth was trembling, like he was about to cry. Blood was trickling from the cut on his lip. As he unclenched his fists, this look of complete vulnerability flooded across his face. He looked about three years old. And lost. Like the world had ended.

Then James and Grace were rushing towards us, along with what felt like half the pub. I glanced round at where Grace was pulling a sobbing Emmi gently to her feet. I looked back at Flynn. The vulnerable look was already gone.

The pub landlord emerged, full of questions about what had happened. We explained that it had been too dark to see the guys' faces. The landlord said he'd noticed them across the bar earlier, but that they weren't regulars. Part of me was relieved. It meant that what had happened was over. No one was hurt, after all.

Except Flynn.

Someone brought him some ice wrapped in a napkin for his cut lip. I held it in place for him, feeling it melt and drip down my hand. As the bustle around us died down, my whole body started shaking.

'Did you see my uppercut?' he grinned. 'It was sound. And with my left hand as well.'

I shook my head. 'Don't,' I said.

Don't make out this was some macho game.

Don't pretend you weren't upset.

He stroked my hair. 'It's okay,' he said. 'It's okay.'

But it wasn't okay.

I started crying and I couldn't stop. It wasn't just the guys who'd grabbed us and what might have happened. It was everything. How I felt about Flynn. How I wanted him to feel about me. It didn't matter how close we were when we were kissing. I needed words. I needed that occasional poem.

I was suddenly aware of how little he'd really told me. Nothing about his parents. Nothing to explain why he was so protective of his sisters. Nothing to explain why he was so angry all the time.

Nothing about how he felt about me.

161

The minicab Grace had ordered came. She and James put me and Emmi inside with Flynn. He looked slightly panic-stricken at the prospect – we were still crying our eyes out. But there wasn't enough room for both Grace and James to travel with us, so they stayed behind.

I knew James had pressed some money into Flynn's hands to pay for the cab. And I knew Flynn was annoyed about it, which infuriated me. For God's sake. How could he carry on being so uptight about money after what had just happened? Surely getting me and Emmi home quickly was more important than who was paying for the cab?

Inside the taxi, Flynn put his arm round me. My irritation increased. I started to feel the weight of his hand like a clamp. I peered round him. Emmi was curled up against the far door still weeping quietly.

'D'you think she's all right?' Flynn whispered.

Why was he so concerned about Emmi? I'd been attacked too.

As soon as I'd thought this, I felt guilty. Emmi was in a total state and, if I was honest, what had happened earlier had been worse for her.

'Emmi?' I said softly. 'Are you okay?'

Emmi nodded, but she didn't turn round and she didn't stop crying.

I glanced at Flynn. He was still watching Emmi,

looking concerned. A mean sliver of jealousy lodged itself in my head.

I shrugged. 'You try,' I said, pulling away from him.

Flynn frowned at me, but he leaned over and put his hand on Emmi's shoulder. 'Emmi?'

She whipped round, her face glistening with tears, and flung herself against his chest, wrapping her arms around him and sobbing even louder than she had before.

Flynn stared down at her in horror, then did the only thing he could do. He put his arms gently around her.

'Hey, Emmi,' he said soothingly. 'You're safe. It's okay. You're safe – it's all over.'

I glared at them, furious now, unable to speak.

I desperately wanted Flynn to push her away, to turn back to me. It was irrational and unkind – but I couldn't help it. I'd pictured them holding each other so often, in their roles as Romeo and Juliet, hating the images of them together that forced themselves into my head. And now, here they both were, halfway to a full-on kissing session.

And it was all my fault for pushing Flynn towards her.

Knowing that made me feel even angrier. Emmi didn't stop crying all the way home, and she

163

didn't let go of Flynn either. He turned several times and looked at me apologetically. A couple of times he tried to reach out to hold me too. But I shrank away. No way was he getting his hands on both of us.

I said as little as possible when we reached Emmi's house. We helped her in through the front door and, as her parents barely knew Flynn and as Emmi was still sobbing and incoherent, they fell on me, demanding to know what had happened.

As I explained, the full weight of the situation hit home. My guts tensed up at the thought of how much danger we'd been in. How terrifying the whole thing had been.

But no one seemed to notice me. After I'd finished explaining, Emmi's mum flapped hysterically round her daughter while her dad pushed Flynn – rather aggressively – to describe in detail how he'd dealt with the two guys who'd harassed us.

By the time we got inside the next cab I was all knotted up, seething with a rage that I didn't understand. I mean, I wasn't in danger any more. The whole episode was over, wasn't it?

Flynn told the driver my address, then slumped back on the back seat with a deep sigh.

'Man, that was heavy,' he groaned. He turned to me and scooped his arm round my shoulders. I sat, rigidly, while he dropped his head and kissed the back of my neck.

'River?' He straightened up, pulling me closer. 'What's wrong?'

I don't know. That would have been the honest answer. I felt like a pressure cooker, all these big emotions swirling around in my head and no way of letting them go. But I couldn't think how to put that into words, so I said nothing.

Flynn sat back with a sigh. 'I hope Emmi's all right,' he said. 'Those pigs really freaked her out.'

Emmi. Again. My feelings of anger solidified around that one point and the sliver of jealousy that slid inside me earlier exploded into a thousand shards, each one full of hate.

'Getting in practice for your Big Performance?' I said sarcastically.

'What?' Flynn stared at me.

I could see in his face he had no idea what I was talking about. Or else he was acting. It suddenly struck me that he was such a brilliant actor I would never know if he was lying. Ever.

The thought was not comforting.

'Enjoy getting close to Emmi on the way home?' I hissed.

I knew that was totally unfair, but I couldn't help myself.

Flynn made a face at me. 'Don't be stupid, Riv.' He frowned, as if waiting for me to say sorry and snuggle up to him.

It was what I wanted to do. But the angry, jealous, hateful knives inside me wouldn't let me. I stared back at him, waiting for him to say that it was me he wanted. That he'd rather eat dog poo than kiss Emmi.

But he didn't.

'Look, River,' he sighed. 'I'm sure you're feeling like crap, but frankly so am I. Okay? So why don't you cut out this rubbish about Emmi and tell me what's really wrong?' His voice was calm, but I recognised the steely anger underneath.

It infuriated me.

'You don't let me in,' I said. 'I mean, you let me in so far and then no further.'

'What the hell are you talking about?'

'Your past. Your mum and dad. Your drinking – or lack of it. Your attitude to money. To Siobhan. I mean, I've never even been to your house, Flynn.' The words were spitting out of me. 'I want you to trust me.'

Flynn rolled his eyes. 'Give it a chance, Riv,' he said. 'We've only been going out a few weeks.'

'So what?' I was shouting now. 'Romeo and Juliet only met a few times and they were prepared to die for—'

'OH, SHUT *UP* ABOUT THAT FRIGGING PLAY,' Flynn roared. 'IT'S FRIGGING FICTION, RIVER. MADE UP. PEOPLE'S REAL LIVES AREN'T LIKE THAT.'

He swung away from me across the back seat of the cab.

Tears welled in my eyes. I glanced up at the cab driver. He was studiously ignoring us, staring steadily out of the front window.

A great pit of fear and loneliness opened up in my stomach. I had a flashback to that moment of utter panic earlier, when the fair-haired guy had dragged me across the alleyway. For two or three seconds I'd been so scared. And Flynn had saved me. And been hurt doing it. And here I was yelling at him.

I wriggled across the back seat and put my hand on his arm. 'Flynn?'

He was stiff, unyielding. I could feel the anger still pulsing through him.

'I'm sorry,' I said. 'I know I'm being weird. It's just I . . . I was so frightened earlier. I thought those guys were really going to . . . to attack us.'

It wasn't the full reason I'd got jealous and pushed Flynn to open up, but I was pretty sure it was the only explanation of my behaviour that would get us to a hug in the next two minutes.

With a sigh Flynn turned round.

'I just can't handle a frigging tantrum right now, okay?' he mumbled.

I looked up at his face. A bruise was developing around the cut on his lip where the guy in the alleyway had punched him. It felt like that moment had happened a million years ago. I stroked the red, swollen skin around the cut.

The cab stopped at some traffic lights. A street lamp outside cast a pale glow over Flynn's face. His eyes were so full of feeling – a great mixture of longing and fear and hurt and anger.

'I don't want to go home,' I whispered. 'Please can I come back to your house?'

Flynn stared at me for a long time. And then his eyes clouded over.

'I've never taken anyone home,' he said slowly. 'Anyone. Ever.'

I caught my breath. My heart pounded.

'I'm not anyone.' I hesitated, and the words – unplanned and unprompted – bled out of me. 'I love you.'

There was a long pause, then he bent his head closer and whispered in my ear.

'I'm sorry.'

He sat back, not touching me.

We spent the rest of the journey in silence. I felt totally numb. I'd expected that once I said I loved

168

him, he would automatically say it back. I'd imagined that once I asked, straight out, for him to trust me and talk to me and take me home, he would. That the way we felt about each other – the strength of it, the passion of it – would burn everything else away.

By the time we reached my house, I had to face that I'd been wrong. I'd misunderstood how he felt. Flynn was just an intelligent boy with a chip on his shoulder about being poor, a headful of hormones that made him good at kissing and a fierce desire to grow up to be rich.

There was nothing beyond that. Or nothing he wanted to share with me, anyway.

He wasn't in love with me.

He wasn't Romeo.

18

Mum gasped when she saw my tear-stained face and Flynn's cut lip. Again, I explained what had happened. Flynn stood sullenly beside me, making eye contact with neither of us. It was obvious he couldn't wait to leave. He said goodbye without a kiss. Just squeezed my arm, then went.

I stumbled upstairs while Mum flapped and fussed and ran me a hot bath.

She tried to get me to talk about what had happened at the pub. But beyond reassuring her that I wasn't hurt and that the whole thing had only lasted a couple of minutes, I refused to talk.

She left me to get some sleep.

But sleep wouldn't come.

The next day was Thursday. I told Mum I couldn't face school.

The truth was, I couldn't face the rehearsal.

Couldn't face Flynn.

I had no way of contacting him, I realised. He had no mobile and he'd never given me a home phone number either. He said his family didn't have a phone line.

Yeah, right.

I took this as further proof that he didn't really care about me – and sank into a dark, bottomless misery.

Emmi phoned that evening, but I didn't want to speak to her either. I still felt angry with her for crying all over Flynn in the cab. Perhaps if she hadn't done that, I wouldn't have got so angry myself and . . .

No. In my heart I knew it wasn't Emmi's fault.

I still didn't want to speak to her, though. She was his Juliet. And I was nothing.

Mum let me stay off school on Friday as well. Normally I'd see Flynn on a Friday evening, but he hadn't called and, anyway, there was no way I could go out with him now. I couldn't bear loving him so much and knowing he didn't feel the same.

I lounged about the house all weekend, hoping that he'd call. Mum started to get seriously worried about me, nagging me to eat and asking why I wasn't going out with Emmi and Grace. She even suggested that I spoke to a counsellor about the attack at the pub.

I told her I was fine and pretended I was going off to meet Emmi.

As I reached the park, Emmi herself rang again. I took the call this time, in case she decided to phone my home number if I didn't.

We chatted for a bit, then Emmi asked how Flynn was. I told her I thought things were cooling off between us.

'No way,' Emmi said. 'I mean I still think he's too intense, but he obviously cares about you. Why else would he have come to our defence like that?'

Because he trains to fight in that boxing club. Because being angry is who he is.

I said nothing. Just ended the call and walked, shivering, round the park. It was a bitterly cold day. The first of December. There would only be a couple more weeks of rehearsals. And then the two performances.

Not long to go. Not long before I'd never see Flynn again.

Dad was there when I got back from the park. Mum and Stone went out of the room and left us drinking a cup of tea in the kitchen.

We sat in silence for a while. Dad looked so out of place in our house now – with his fuzzy beard and his shapeless cord trousers. It was funny to think he'd once lived here.

'You haven't come to see me for a while,' he said.

There was no reproach in his voice. Just a mild curiosity. I said nothing.

Dad drained his cup and set it down on the table. 'So,' he said slowly. 'What's up?'

I shrugged.

Dad sat there, waiting.

But this time, I didn't want to speak to him. So I sat there too, not saying anything.

Dad cleared his throat. 'Okay. You don't want to talk. That's fine. I just wanted you to know I'm here, if you need me.'

He stood up.

'Dad?' My voice was small and broken. A hot tear leaked out of my eye.

Dad came over and put his arms round me. I breathed in his familiar smell – musty clothes and earth and a hint of incense.

'Dad, he doesn't love me.' My voice broke as I said the words out loud. 'He's all closed in and hidden away and I've tried, but he won't let me in and I don't know what I did wrong and oh, Daddy, I can't bear it . . .'

He hugged me tighter as I sobbed. Stroking my hair. Letting me cry it all out. 'You've done nothing wrong,' he kept saying. 'Let it go . . . let it go . . .'

He held me for what felt like a long time, just stroking my hair.

And when I looked up, his eyes were bright, like jewels.

Like he'd been crying too.

I went to back to school on Monday, feeling stronger. I stayed strong all day – telling Emmi and Grace it was definitely over with Flynn. I stayed strong all the way to St Cletus's, in fact.

And then I walked into the assembly room and saw him on the stage. And I wanted to die. He was rehearsing Act 5, when Romeo mistakenly thinks that Juliet is dead.

Mr Nichols ordered Emmi up on stage, so Flynn had a real person to work with. I watched him run his hands down the outline of her body – almost touching her but not quite.

'Death, that hath suck'd the honey of thy breath
Hath had no power yet upon thy beauty.'

And Emmi did look beautiful lying there.

I listened to him say his lines, lost in the intensity of his misery. I left before he could talk to me afterwards. The next day I phoned and left a message for Mr Nichols, saying I was too ill to come to rehearsals for the rest of the week.

I planned another quiet weekend. I went out shopping with Emmi and Grace after school on Friday.

174

We came back late afternoon – Emmi and Grace rushed off to get ready for a party they were both set on going to. I told them I might come by later and pretended I was going to check out a skirt I'd spotted in one of the local shops. Then I hung around the High Street until six o'clock. I knew that was when Siobhan normally finished her shift at the hairdressers'. I waited over the road for Flynn to arrive.

He was there at two minutes to – just a hint of a swagger in the way he strolled up to the shop and leaned against the lamp post outside. He put his hands in his pockets, then lifted one foot and rested the sole against the lamp post behind him.

He didn't look round. He didn't see me.

I watched him hungrily. The street was still fairly busy and I could see his head turning, every now and then, gazing at the people who passed him. It started raining – a few light drops. Flynn looked up at the sky, his fringe falling away from his forehead. He folded his arms, muttering something. He was only wearing a thin cotton top. I smiled, imagining him saying *frigging weather* under his breath.

Then Siobhan came out. She looked straight across the road before I had a chance to duck back. For a second I thought she'd seen me – but she didn't wave or anything and Flynn didn't turn round, so I guessed she hadn't.

They walked off together, deep in conversation. I watched them go, a million feelings careering around my head: how much I wanted to speak to Flynn myself . . . how much I envied his sister right now . . . and how much I missed him, like a big dark hole at the very heart of me.

I stopped at the park entrance on the way home. The light rain had stopped and the wind was getting up. I didn't want Mum to see I'd been crying. But my plan to let the chilly December air cool off my tear-stained face didn't work. As I leaned against the park gates, my whole face crumpled. Every cell of my body cried out for him.

I bent over, trying to hold in the agony of it.

'Don't cry.' Flynn's voice was clear and strong, and right beside me.

I whipped round. He was standing less than a metre away, his lion eyes glinting in the street light.

My hands sprang to my face, furiously wiping away my tears.

Flynn moved closer. 'Siobhan saw you just now,' he said. 'She wouldn't let me get on the bus with her. Told me to come after you.'

I looked up at him, my heart pounding. The wind was tearing past us, fierce and raw on my face.

'Oh yeah?' I said, trying to keep my voice steady. 'You don't normally do what you're told.'

He smiled. 'Siobhan said I was being an idiot. She said that if you really liked me, you wouldn't care where we lived or who our family was. That if I was ashamed of it, that was my problem. Not yours.'

'Oh.' I hesitated. 'That's funny. My dad said the same thing. More or less.'

'Yeah, well.' His grin deepened. 'Dropouts. Hairstylists. What do they know?'

I stared at him. *God*, he looked beautiful. Why did he have to look so beautiful? I could feel my face starting to crumple again. I didn't want this. Not him standing this close and laughing like it was no big deal and me wanting him so much I couldn't breathe.

It started raining again. We stood there, letting it fall on our faces.

Then Flynn's eyes softened. 'I can't stop thinking about you.'

My heart seemed to squeeze up into my throat. Everything stopped. The hiss of the distant traffic, the patter of the rain, the wind in the trees behind us. It just faded away into the other universe.

The one without Flynn.

'Can we go back to the other night?' he said. 'When you asked to come back to my place. D'you remember?'

I nodded. *Of course I do.*

'D'you remember what I said next?'

I nodded again. 'That you'd never taken anyone home. Ever.'

Flynn moved closer, so that he was standing just centimetres away from me. A drop of rain trickled off his fringe and rolled down his face.

'And then your line was: *I'm not anyone. I love you.* Which was a great line. Only . . .' He bent his head, so that our noses were almost touching. 'I messed my next line up,' he sighed. 'I just said *I'm sorry.*'

The whole world shrank to his eyes.

'So what should you have said?' I whispered.

He smiled. 'I should have said: *Okay then, come home with me. Then we'll see if you love me.*'

19

It was six-thirty by the time the bus dropped us at Archway. We walked round the corner and down the Holloway Road, where I knew Flynn lived.

The road was busy and dirty and full of traffic and litter. I could feel Flynn tensing as we walked. We'd hardly talked on the bus. It was like we were in limbo.

Waiting.

My heart thumped as I followed Flynn down an endless row of boarded-up newsagent's, sex shops and convenience stores. He finally stopped at a set of steps sandwiched between a bleak, harshly-lit café and a cheap-looking estate agency. The door at the top of the steps had six buzzers beside it. I could only count four windows above our heads.

Flynn turned his key in the lock and pushed the door open. The smell of damp was overpowering.

He banged his fist against some kind of switch on the wall. A light flickered on and off overhead.

Flynn swore under his breath. Then he strode across to a staircase opposite the door and started climbing. The smell of damp receded as we reached the second floor. There were three doors leading off the tiny landing. Flynn turned to the one on the right and fitted his key.

I followed him inside, my hands shaking. I don't know why I was so scared. I just knew that what we were doing was a very big deal.

A threadbare carpet led away from the door for a few metres. Two doors on the left. Two on the right.

'This won't take long,' Flynn said darkly. He opened the first door on the right. It was a bathroom – a tiny bath on one side, a loo and a sink on the other. He shut the door quickly. I only had time to get a general impression. Messy but clean.

He opened the next door. A living room – if you could call it that – about three metres square, with three beanbags on the floor, a TV and a tiny, spotless kitchen area to the right. I noticed a pile of Flynn's school books in the corner. For some reason the sight of them brought a lump to my throat.

Flynn shut the door. 'Had enough?'

I shook my head. He leaned over and opened the

first of the doors on the left of the tiny corridor. Siobhan was lying asleep, her red hair spread out on the pillow of the double bed which took up most of the room. There was a single chest of drawers on the far wall and a small clothes rail crammed with clothes. I could make out less than half a square metre of carpet between the bed and the door.

'She always sleeps for a bit when she gets in from work,' Flynn whispered. 'She says Mum snores and it keeps her awake at night.'

He closed the door quietly and moved on to the next room.

It was even smaller than the first bedroom. Someone had hung a curtain down the middle of the room. The near side of the curtain contained a single mattress covered with a faded Barbie duvet cover. A couple of cardboard boxes containing clothes and toys stood against the curtain. There were only a few centimetres between the boxes and the mattress – about the width of a child's foot.

'This is Caitlin's,' Flynn said.

He took a single step across the room to the curtain, then twitched it back and waved me through. 'My room,' he said sarcastically. I crept past him. A single mattress lay on the floor against

181

the far wall. Books and magazines and clothes were scattered all over the remaining floor space. The entire area was about two and a half metres long by one and a half metres wide.

My mouth fell open. I looked back, out to the corridor and the other rooms. The whole flat had to be the size of our living room.

I didn't know how to meet Flynn's eyes. There was a long silence. Then he shoved his hands in his pockets and stepped over to the door.

'D'you want me to walk you down to the bus stop?' he said dully.

I didn't move. I stood staring down at the little mattress, at all the mess. I caught sight of his copy of *Romeo and Juliet*, lying open on the window sill above the mattress. I stepped over and picked up the book. Romeo's lines were marked:

Heaven is here
Where Juliet lives. And every cat and dog
And little mouse, every unworthy thing
Live here in heaven and may look on her:
But Romeo may not.

I sank down onto the mattress and switched on the little light that stood on the floor beside it.

The floor creaked. I looked up. Flynn was staring down at me. There was so much hurt in his eyes I couldn't bear it.

Tears welled up, and the lump in my throat grew painful. I had had so many questions about his home a few days before. And now I was here, none of them seemed important any more.

Flynn came and sat beside me. He took the book from my hands.

'I thought if you saw who I was,' he said in a low voice, 'you wouldn't want me.'

I shook my head, and lay down, pulling him onto the mattress beside me. A tear rolled down my cheek. Flynn bent across and kissed it away.

We lay without speaking for a long time. My head rested on Flynn's chest. His hand stroked my hair. I smiled to myself. I loved the way we could do that – just be together without having to fill the space between us with words. Knowing that the words were coming.

After a while, Flynn took a deep breath.

'My dad's a drunk.' His voice was steady, but I could hear all the layers of feeling behind what he was saying – the anger and the hurt and the humili-ation. I lay where I was, sensing he didn't want me to look at him while he was speaking.

'He's from some town near Birmingham. Met my mum when she was sixteen and he was on holiday in Ireland,' Flynn went on. 'He was older. Good-looking. Full of big promises. Then she got pregnant with Siobhan. Her family kicked her out – you know. Strict Catholics. Tiny village in Ireland. Big frigging scandal. So they came over here. He worked as a labourer for a while. His drinking got worse. And then Siobhan was born. Mum got pregnant with me almost straight away. So there they were. Two kids. No money. My dad lost his job cos of his drinking. My mum started doing cleaning jobs, trying to make ends meet. I remember going with her when I was little. All these snooty cows she worked for looking down at her. A teenage girl with two kids. Shacked up with the local drunk.' He ground his teeth. 'Talk about a frigging cliché.'

I lay very still, my heart pounding.

Flynn took a deep breath. 'So on it went. Mum got pregnant again. Lost the baby. Then one day my dad just left. No word. No goodbye. I guess I was about three or four. We didn't see him for years. I don't know why. I remember him coming back, though. This big dark stranger who smelled funny – all sweaty with horrible breath. He moved back in. None of us wanted him there, but Mum was scared. I mean, she must have been scared before, but now I was older I could see it in her eyes.' He paused. 'Anyway, they had Caitlin. My dad just lounged around the house all day. Drinking

184

while Mum was out working. I remember coming home from school, him shouting and staggering about . . .'

Flynn fell silent. I wondered if he was going to say any more. I wanted to hug him, to hold him and tell him how sorry I was.

But something about the way he was holding me, his hand running up and down my arm, told me he was scared of me feeling sorry for him. That the one thing I mustn't do was pity him.

After a long pause, Flynn spoke again. And this time his voice trembled with anger.

'He started knocking Mum about. Slaps and shoves at first. Then worse. I wasn't really aware of what was going on. I mean, not how bad it was. Siobhan was, though. She looked after me – she'd take me out of the room if they were arguing. We'd curl up together on the bed and she'd tell me stories about how one day we were going to be very rich and live in a big house and how Mammy and Da would stop fighting and . . .'

'Oh, Flynn.' The words seemed to breathe themselves out of me. Tears were running down my face. I couldn't bear to think of him curled up and frightened – just a little boy. I buried my face in his chest and wept.

He gently stroked my hair again. I sniffed. This

was all wrong. I should be comforting him, not . . .

'By the time I was twelve we were all afraid of him, all the time. He punched my mum so badly once she had to go to hospital. I was scared she wouldn't come back. I don't know why she stayed with him. But I didn't question it at the time. You don't when you're little. You just accept whatever's . . . Anyway, that year I grew about ten centimetres in six months. And I started realising it wasn't normal. That not everyone's da was a loser drunk who hit their mum.'

Flynn sat up and undid the top few buttons of his shirt. He dragged the shirt down over his arm. There, on the ridge of his shoulder, was a puckered white scar. He looked at me for the first time since he'd started talking. 'I tried to stop him hitting Mum,' he said in a dull voice. 'He went mental. Glassed me. If I hadn't been quick, he'd have got my face. Or my throat.'

I blinked, staring at the scar. My head couldn't take in what he was saying – what he must have gone through.

Flynn pulled his shirt up and started rebuttoning it. 'In a way it was a good thing. He'd never touched any of us before. But now it was like him hurting me woke Mum up. She kicked him out, then she went

186

to the police. Dad did some time in jail. When he came out, Mum got a non-molestation order . . .' He tailed off.

I looked up at his face. I could just make out the shadow of the bruise around his mouth from the fight in the pub alleyway. I stroked the tiny scar where his lip had been cut.

'So have you seen your dad since . . . since what happened?'

Flynn leaned his forehead down onto mine. He stopped doing up the buttons on his own shirt and hooked a finger round the top button on mine.

'Yeah, he's not supposed to come near any of us . . . that's what the non-molestation order is for . . . but he does. Asking for money, mostly. That's why I meet Siobhan after work all the time. He knows she's a soft touch – well, compared to me or Mum. Plus, if he's drunk . . .'

He gazed at me for a long time, his eyes searching my face. Then he started unbuttoning my shirt. I didn't stop him. I just sat there while he peeled off my shirt, then lowered his face, kissing my neck, his fingers fumbling with my bra fastening. I arched up, making it easier for him. Then I closed my eyes, feeling him peeling the bra straps down my arms.

'You're so beautiful,' he whispered.

'You make me feel beautiful,' I whispered back.

I lay back while he kissed me, my whole body radiating with how amazing it felt, with how close we were now.

The only sound was our breathing.

Until the noise of a key turning in a lock.

20

My eyes snapped open. 'Flynn?'

He pulled reluctantly away from me. 'That'll be Mum and Caitlin back from Mass.'

'What?' I squeaked, grabbing at my bra. I sat up, fumbling to turn it right side up. 'What were you doing, letting me be all undressed? They could . . .' The words caught in my throat as I imagined them walking straight in. I did up the bra in front, then swivelled it round, hooking my arms through the straps.

'Well, Siobhan was here the whole time . . . you weren't bothered about that.' Flynn rolled his eyes in mock-exasperation.

Oh my God. My stomach lurched. I'd completely forgotten Flynn's sister asleep next door.

Flynn stood up. 'Jesus,' he groaned under his breath. Then he turned and grinned at me. 'We gotta talk about stopping and starting like this, Riv. It's killing me.'

I eyeballed him furiously, as I struggled to straighten one of the bra straps.

Flynn reached over and untwisted it. 'Don't blame me.' He laughed. 'You shouldn't look like you do.' He held up my shirt for me. I poked my arms through the sleeves. As I hauled it round and fumbled for the first button, I heard the bedroom door open.

'Flynn?' It was a little girl's voice.

He disappeared through the curtain.

'I've told you to knock, Caitlin,' he said mock-seriously.

''S my room too,' Caitlin said crossly.

I stood up, fiddling with the bottom button. *There*. I smoothed down my hair.

Flynn poked his head back round the curtain.

'Come and meet Caitlin,' he grinned.

I emerged into Caitlin's section of the room, feeling extremely self-conscious. She was standing by the door, dressed in a long pink skirt and a white T-shirt. She was pretty – about eight or nine – with the same dark red hair as Siobhan – but curly and cut in a short bob. Her pale blue eyes widened into saucers as she saw me.

'This is River,' Flynn said.

Caitlin stared at me.

'Hi, Caitlin,' I said.

She carried on staring. There was something slightly haughty about the way she was looking at me that reminded me of Flynn.

Flynn rolled his eyes. 'Jesus, normally we can't shut you up, Cait. What's your problem?'

Caitlin turned to him. 'Is she your girlfriend?' she asked.

Flynn put his arm round me. 'Oh yes,' he grinned. Then he bent down and whispered in my ear: 'Wait here a minute, I'm just going to tell Mum you're here. She'll freak if we just show. Okay?'

I nodded. I was feeling slightly freaked myself by the entire situation: Flynn's home, his life story and now meeting his sister and his mum. It was all a bit overwhelming. Still, it was what I wanted. My heart soared as I thought of how relaxed Flynn had been with me just before Caitlin walked in. How close to him I'd felt. Closer than ever.

Flynn slipped out of the room, leaving me and Caitlin alone. She was staring at me again. I looked round the room again, trying to think of something to say to her. My eyes lit on the faded Barbie cover stretched neatly over the mattress.

'D'you like Barbie, then?' I said.

'No way.' Caitlin's face screwed up into a contemptuous grimace. 'Not since I was really young,' she said. 'It's a very old duvet cover.'

191

'Yes.' I bit my lip. 'Of course.' I sat down on the floor, remembering where Flynn had said she'd been. 'So you've been to Mass, then?'

She nodded, sitting down opposite me on the mattress.

'What's that like?'

Her eyes widened. 'Don't you go?'

I shook my head. 'Never.'

'What, not *ever*?' Caitlin seemed dumbstruck by this news. 'Not even at Christmas and Easter like Siobhan?'

I shook my head again. 'I'm not Catholic.'

Caitlin nodded. This seemed to make sense to her. 'What's your name? Was it Reeva?'

'River,' I said. 'Like the water.'

Caitlin made another face. 'That's weird,' she said.

I grinned. 'I know,' I said. 'I used to get bullied about it when I was your age.'

Caitlin looked interested. 'Did you tell a teacher?'

'Well . . .'

'Jaysus, Paddy.' A woman's voice across the corridor – an Irish accent. 'What are you doing with the poor girl, keeping her hidden away in your room?'

Footsteps pounded towards us. I caught Caitlin's eye. She grinned.

As the door opened, I scrambled to my feet.

Flynn's mum stood in the doorway. She was slim

and smaller than I'd expected. Only a centimetre or two taller than me with the same red hair as Siobhan and Caitlin. But what struck me most was how tired she looked. Her pale forehead was creased with deep lines and there were dark rings under her eyes.

We blinked at each other for a moment, then Flynn's mum started talking.

'It's grand to meet you, River. I'm so sorry Paddy took you into the room there. I don't know what he was thinking. You didn't want to see all his messy bits and pieces all over the floor . . .'

'I—'

'Come on, now, with me and we'll put on the kettle.'

She gripped me firmly by the elbow and drew me across the corridor and into the little living room/kitchen area. Flynn was sitting on one of the beanbags, his chin propped in his hands, gazing up at us with a slightly bemused expression on his face.

'Now, Paddy,' his mum said. 'Get up and make us a nice cup of tea. Go on with you now. Go on.'

Flynn leaped to his feet and strode towards us, into the little kitchen area near the door. Three of us standing there was a squeeze, so his mum walked across the little carpet and eased herself down onto a beanbag.

I caught Flynn's eye as he filled the kettle under the tap. He was blushing slightly, his expression both amused and embarrassed.

'Sugar?' he said.

I took a step closer to him. 'Thanks, *Paddy*,' I whispered.

I wondered if he remembered how, ages ago, I'd asked him what his family called him. How he'd ignored me, then.

Smiling, he bent down and kissed the side of my head.

'Flynn to you,' he whispered. 'Swampy.'

As he straightened up, I noticed him glance over at his mum. She'd turned the TV on and was tapping her fingers on her lap, very carefully ignoring us.

I turned away from him and stood there awkwardly. His mum looked up and smiled at me again. She patted the beanbag next to her. 'Come and sit down – Flynn's told me a little about you, but not much . . . you know how he is, not a big one for talking.'

I nodded, as she went on.

'River's such a pretty name. I'm Mary, by the way.'

I wandered over and sat down next to her. The bright overhead light cast shadows across her face.

She was almost pretty when she talked – her face lit up and animated. But when she fell silent, as she was now, her face sagged with what seemed like a bone-deep weariness. I realised with a jolt that if she'd only been sixteen or so when she'd had Siobhan, she couldn't be more than thirty-two or -three now. That was fifteen years younger than my mother.

Yet she looked at least ten years older.

'Now, I know you and Paddy met doing the play at his school.' She smiled warmly. 'I'm so pleased he's finally introduced me to a friend of his. I was beginning to think he was ashamed of me. Are you enjoying doing *Romeo and Juliet*?'

'I love it,' I said. 'It's a great play.'

'Oh yes.' She clasped her hands together. 'So romantic. *I will not marry yet; and when I do, I swear it shall be Romeo* . . . That Juliet was a bold piece, wasn't she, talking to her mother like that!'

My mouth must have dropped open.

Flynn's mum laughed. 'Now you didn't think I'd know that, did you? I've been reading Paddy's play to test him on his lines – he's so good in the part and with his school studies and so hard-working. He's going to be a lawyer, you know.'

'Stop it, Mum,' Flynn grunted, walking towards us with a mug of tea in each hand.

His mum beamed up at him as she took one of the mugs.

'Go on with you,' she said. 'You know that you're loving me talking you up to your girl here.' She turned back to me. 'Now, River, you will stay for something to eat, won't you?'

I blinked at her. Stay for dinner? I looked around, wondering where on earth they all ate. There was no sign of a table and no space for chairs. There would barely be room for all four of them to sit down on the three beanbags as it was.

'We eat out of tins,' Flynn said solemnly. 'Sometimes just out of our hands. It saves washing up.'

'Paddy.' His mum flapped her hands at him exasperatedly. 'Get off with you. Leave River here to help me with the tea. Go and do some of that homework you're always complaining you don't get enough time to—'

'I don't complain,' Flynn grinned. 'I—'

'Go *on*.'

And he went.

I stood at the kitchen counter with his mum peeling potatoes. Her hands were red raw and chafed. She yawned constantly as she worked, in between keeping up a non-stop chatter about her jobs and her two girls. I learned that Caitlin was good at school, but lazy and prone to answer back 'like her brother', Flynn's mum said darkly. And I picked up that, like Flynn, she worried about Siobhan. She didn't exactly say so, but her whole face grew concerned as she told me how hard Siobhan found talking to people.

Flynn's mum asked me questions too. Subtle ones about my family – I found myself saying how difficult it was to talk to my mum, how close I felt to my dad – and I'm sure she realised how I felt about Flynn. I went bright red whenever she mentioned him.

She talked about him proudly, telling me how well he'd done in his GCSEs.

Once the potatoes were on, she took a pot out of the tiny fridge and set it on the gas cooker. It was some kind of stew. A bit of meat, padded out with loads of pearl barley and carrots, she said. Flynn reappeared just before it was ready. He glanced anxiously over at me.

Are you OK?

I smiled back.

Flynn was sent to fetch Siobhan and Caitlin and we all sat down on the living room floor to eat. It was weird. The TV blared out the whole time, a permanent background noise. There was no table. No chairs. None of the plates matched and there weren't even enough proper forks to go round, so Caitlin had to use a spoon. And yet it was a real family meal. Warm and chatty and full of laughter.

At my house I was used to hardly speaking to Mum – and Stone just grunted when anyone talked to him. Here everyone chattered on non-stop. Flynn and Caitlin teased each other all the time. Even Siobhan joined in occasionally, accusing Flynn of borrowing her hair wax that morning. Flynn's mum kept it all together, never letting the conversation get too mean or aggressive, her eyes flickering about from plate to plate, looking horrified at Caitlin shovelling her food down in huge mouthfuls, then concerned as Siobhan picked listlessly at hers.

I noticed how carefully she'd measured out the delicious stew. She took hardly any for herself, then gave Siobhan a little more. Caitlin and I both got bigger portions. But the lion's share was reserved for Flynn – not only did he get by far the biggest helping but also, I was sure, the one with most actual meat in it.

I tried to make his mum take some of the stew on my plate, but she refused so adamantly that I didn't dare push it. I sat back, savouring each guilty mouthful and watching the others, especially Flynn.

I loved how they all adored him. You could see how much Caitlin looked up to him. How Siobhan relied on him. And as for his mum – well, it was obvious to me after about five minutes of watching them together, that while she might love her daughters, Flynn was utterly and completely the centre of her universe.

There was only one moment when I glimpsed any major tension between them and that was when Flynn's mum started telling me about Caitlin's first Holy Communion, which had apparently been postponed from last summer when Caitlin was ill and was now coming up after Christmas. She talked as if she assumed I knew what a first Holy Communion was. In fact, I had no idea, but I listened and nodded politely.

After a minute or two she said, 'So do you ever go to Mass, River?'

'Jesus, Mum,' Flynn snapped, a real edge to his voice. 'No, she frigging doesn't.'

'Watch your language,' his mum snapped back. She stared down at her plate, clearly hurt. I looked round helplessly. Siobhan had suddenly become transfixed by whatever was on the TV. Flynn was staring at his mum, his expression half angry, half guilty.

Caitlin, however, was grinning. 'River's not even Catholic,' she said archly.

Flynn's mum's head shot up, her eyes wide with

shock. 'But I thought with the play, with the schools getting together that . . .' She glanced at Flynn who was glowering at her, clearly restraining himself with difficulty from snapping at her again.

'My school's not a religious school,' I said quickly. 'In fact, I don't really have a religion at all. Well, I think my mum's parents might have been Jewish, but I don't know any more about that than . . .' I stopped. They were all staring at me. I looked at Flynn. *What?*

He grinned at me as if I'd just made the funniest joke, ever.

'There you go, Mum, she's Jewish,' he said.

Siobhan beside me gave a little snort of laughter.

Their mum blinked for a second, then beamed at me. 'Don't listen to them, River,' she said. 'It doesn't matter in the slightest what religion you are, they just like to tease me.'

We finished eating, then Flynn cleared away the plates. As he strode over to the sink and started washing up, Siobhan nudged me in the ribs. 'He's showing off for you,' she whispered. 'He wouldn't normally wash up.'

Flynn's mum stood up, yawning. 'It's all right, Paddy. Why don't you take two minutes to tidy up next door, then maybe you and River would like to do some studying together.'

'Thanks, Mum.' Flynn came over and hugged her. She looked tiny in his arms. She whispered something in his ear. He rolled his eyes, then winked at me over her shoulder and vanished.

'Now, Caitlin,' his mum went on. 'You can stay here and help me. I've not got work tonight and there's a programme you'll like on in a minute.'

One minute later Flynn reappeared. 'All tidy now,' he announced. He grabbed my hand and whisked me back into the room he shared with Caitlin. I giggled as he pulled me behind the curtain and dragged me onto the mattress. I looked around. His attempt at tidying up seemed to have consisted of picking up the clothes on the floor and hurling them into a single pile in the corner, and stacking up a precarious tower of books and magazines against the only available wall space.

Flynn tugged me further down onto the mattress and leaned over me.

'God,' he whispered, 'I thought I'd never get you away from her.' He grinned. 'So, what did you think?'

I smiled at him. 'They're all great,' I whispered back. I was pretty sure he hadn't shut the bedroom door, and I didn't want them to overhear me. 'Siobhan was less shy than before. And Caitlin's sweet and your mum's lovely. Really kind and welcoming and warm.'

Flynn beamed at me. 'She likes you,' he said, bending down and nibbling my ear. 'I know she does.'

'Yeah, well she freakin' worships you,' I said, closing my eyes as he ran his hand down my shirt.

His face was warm against my cheek. 'I know,' he said.

'Big-head,' I said, thumping him gently on the arm.

'Mmmn.' Flynn kissed my mouth hungrily, flicking the top button of my shirt open with one hand. He rolled slightly more over me, pushing my legs apart with his knee. 'God, I meant that about starting and stopping Riv, I can't . . .'

I suddenly remembered the open door and how close the other rooms in the flat were.

'Stop it.' I pushed his hand away, pulling my shirt together. 'You haven't even shut the door.'

'Can't.' Flynn grimaced, moving his hand down to the bottom of my shirt and expertly undoing the button there. 'It was Mum's condition of me having you in here. She's not used to me having girls round.'

We carried on for a bit, kissing and touching each other, but as soon as Flynn started trying to take off my bra again I pushed his hand away. 'I can't take off my clothes with your mum and sisters a couple of metres away,' I hissed.

He drew back again and grinned at me. 'You know you might as *well* be a freakin' Catholic.'

He rolled onto his back with a sigh.

'Okay then, you big prude,' he said. 'I suppose you want to talk.'

I snuggled against his chest, snaking my arm across his muscular stomach. I sighed contentedly. 'You're like a different person here,' I said. 'Like with tidying your space and not shutting the door. I can't imagine you doing that for anyone else. I mean, look how rude you are to Mr Nichols.'

'I don't think Mr Nichols is all that bothered about my sex life,' Flynn said with a grin.

'You know what I mean.' I squeezed his arm. 'You're different with your mum and Siobhan and Caitlin. Less . . . less angry somehow. More relaxed.'

He looked sideways at me. 'I'm not very relaxed right now, River. Can't we just . . .'

'No,' I said. I sat up and fastened my buttons.

He lay on his back looking up at me. His eyes were laughing and yearning and so hot I felt as if I was melting.

'I want to make love with you,' he said.

'Yeah, right, Flynn.' I laughed. 'The door's open.'

He sat up and held my hand. 'I mean it.' His eyes

burned into me. 'Not here. Not now. But soon. I want to be with you. Properly.'

My heart skipped a beat as I realised what he meant. I stared at him, my mind whirling.

'Telling you everything, tonight, it's like this wall's come down.' Flynn squeezed my hand. 'I've never felt like this about anyone, Riv. You drive me crazy. Like when we were eating earlier, all I could think about was how you looked when I took your top off. And when we're kissing and touching and . . .' He leaned closer to me. 'I don't want to stop,' he said hoarsely. 'I want to feel all of you. With all of me. It's what's supposed to happen.'

My heart pounded. 'I don't know,' I said slowly. I couldn't think straight. I wanted him. I knew I did. But it was too sudden. We'd only just made up after that fight in the minicab and now here he was, zooming into tenth gear.

Flynn took my hand and pressed it against his cheek, his own hand on top. His hand totally swamped mine. I couldn't even see my wrist under his.

'What don't you know?' he said. 'I've opened up to you. Told you everything.'

No you haven't. You haven't told me you love me.

'It's a bit soon,' I mumbled. 'We've only been going out a few weeks.'

Flynn raised his eyebrows at me. 'Romeo and Juliet got married in less time.' He pulled my hand across his face and kissed the palm, very gently.

Trust him. Trust Flynn to use my own words against me.

'Can't you shut up about that frigging play,' I whispered.

I felt his mouth turn up, into a grin, as he kissed his way down to my wrist. I shivered. He felt so good. So right. I loved him more than I could put into words.

And yet it was too soon. Too rushed. It wasn't enough just knowing things about him, I realised. I needed to trust how he felt. I needed the proof that he felt about me like I did about him. That he wasn't going to storm off again over nothing.

I needed to be sure he loved me.

21

After about an hour, Flynn's mum suggested he should walk me down to the bus stop. While he went to the bathroom, she drew me to one side.

'I'm glad he's seeing you,' she smiled.

I smiled shyly back at her.

She sighed. 'He works so hard and makes out he's so tough. And God help you if you suggest that he might not be able to make it all on his own, but underneath there's a part of him that's hurting. You know?'

I nodded, swallowing.

'And that hurting makes him angry. Every time he goes out I worry that he'll do something stupid. You know, give out to someone who upsets him or get in a fight.' She rolled her eyes. 'When I saw his face after that thing with you and your friend . . .' She put her hand on my arm. 'Not that I'm saying he was wrong to step in. But sometimes it *isn't* the right thing to do. Sometimes it's better to walk away. And I worry he won't know how, and then . . . and then all his big dreams'll come crashing down and . . .'

Flynn appeared from the bathroom.

'Ready?' he said.

'Sure.' I looked at his mum.

'Bye, River,' she said. 'Look after yourself – and Paddy. All right?'

That day changed everything between me and Flynn. I felt closer to him than ever. And yet . . . I felt he was pushing me over sex in that intense way he did everything. It wasn't that I didn't want to do it. I did. I *really* did. But I didn't want to rush it.

Part of me wished I could be like Emmi. To her, sex was just another thing – an ordinary, everyday thing. But to me – with Flynn – it had to be perfect.

We met that weekend, on Sunday, and spent the whole afternoon on our own in the park. It was so cold we could see our breath in front of our faces.

Flynn had swallowed his pride and brought the jacket his mum had bought him for two pounds. It *was* pretty disgusting – fake leather with a thick grey lining. He didn't put it on until we were completely out of sight of any other people. Then he wrapped it round us both and we kissed for hours.

207

Kissed and talked. About his family. About his dad. About the times his dad had turned up drunk at the flat – or followed Flynn and Siobhan after school – or threatened Flynn's mum where she worked. I held him tightly, knowing that he'd never told anyone any of these things before.

We talked about the play. I was nervous about having an audience. He wasn't. There were just a couple more days of rehearsals, then the dress rehearsal on Wednesday, with the performances on the Thursday and Friday.

We talked about doing it, too. Well, I did. I had to.

It was dark and we'd gone down to the part of the park that was furthest from the road. A disused stone fountain stood in the middle of a little square, surrounded by four park benches.

We lay down on one of the benches and kissed and touched. Flynn told me again that he wanted to make love. I said I wanted to wait.

'But *why*?' Flynn groaned, pressing against me. 'It's the right thing to do,' he kept saying. 'The next thing. The only thing.'

I couldn't see it like that. I wanted him. But I wanted more time, too. In the end I told him I just wanted to wait until the play was over. He accepted that, and we wandered home, our arms wrapped round each other.

I told myself I was blissfully happy, but in a tiny corner of my brain this little voice was saying, *Why's it going to be different after the play, River? What's going to have changed in five days?*

The next few days were really busy. Mr Nichols was in a terrible mood – he spent most of Monday's rehearsal shouting at anyone who forgot their lines or laughed in the wrong place.

I could see Flynn was on the verge of losing it. Of just walking out on the whole thing. But he somehow managed to keep his temper in check. I knew he was going through his scenes on autopilot – partly because his lines lacked the same level of feeling I'd seen before and partly because it was so obvious what was really on his mind whenever he looked over at me. Still, Flynn on autopilot was better than most of the other actors in the play put together.

To be honest, I felt quite sorry for Mr Nichols. Apart from Emmi and Flynn and Alex, no one really spoke naturally or moved confidently around the stage. Grace constantly forgot her lines. Daisy remembered hers, but was never standing in the right place. And as for James Molloy – he seemed to have lost what little confidence he'd once had, and couldn't be heard from a metre in front of the stage, let alone at the back of the assembly hall.

'It seats five hundred people,' Mr Nichols roared. 'How are they going to hear you IF YOU WHISPER?'

Poor James went bright red and did his next scene even quieter.

By Wednesday's dress rehearsal Mr Nichols had started to lose his voice from all the shouting and was staggering around backstage clutching his throat and whispering last-minute directions at anyone who would stand still long enough to listen to them.

I saw him draw Flynn and Emmi to one side and my heart sank. I knew he must be telling them it was time to put some real kisses in place.

I asked Emmi, very casually, afterwards what Mr Nichols had said.

'Don't use tongues,' she said solemnly.

I stared at her. 'What?'

She grinned. 'I'm kidding. He said we should just see the kisses as part of the lines – and we should ignore anyone who laughs.'

During the dress rehearsal, I stood in the wings, anxiously watching the scene in which Romeo and Juliet meet. Despite what Flynn said I knew he was a little nervous. It was making him act better. He was speaking with real feeling.

As Emmi fluttered out, it struck me how well suited they were. Attractive. Charismatic. Massively up for sex. I'd had those thoughts before, of course, but right now it was particularly hard to see them, all dressed up in their elegant costumes, circling round each other.

My mind went back to that first rehearsal, when Flynn and I had answered all Mr Nichols' questions about what Romeo and Juliet's lines meant. These were *our* lines, I thought jealously.

I stood, hidden by the curtains, waiting for the kiss. I was so intent on the scene in front of me I didn't notice the other people gathering until two of the girls with non-speaking parts from the year below me at school started whispering behind me.

'Will they kiss each other for real?' one of them hissed.

'Course,' the other replied. 'Flynn will, anyway. Look at him – he *so* fancies her.'

'Sssh.' The first girl glanced sideways at me and sniggered.

Out of the corner of my eye, I could see both girls, hands over their mouths, red-faced, suppressing more giggles as they tried not to look at me.

My whole being burned with humiliation. On stage, Flynn was tracing his fingers down Emmi's face. It was a simple gesture – soft and tender – and one he'd often made with me. His eyes were so full of love, so intense. I could hardly believe he was acting. My guts seemed to hollow out as he leaned forwards and brushed his lips against hers.

This wasn't supposed to be how it ended. Emmi was supposed to be ill so that I could go on in her place and he would be my Romeo and I would be his Juliet.

I remembered how Emmi had clung to him in our minicab after the fight in the pub alleyway. Jealousy rose inside me like a dark, thick poison, choking me.

I watched, helplessly, as they drew apart, still gazing into each other's eyes.

The next line was my own cue.

I walked onto the stage. *'Madam, your mother craves a word with you.'* My voice sounded hollow to my ears.

'What is her mother?' Flynn spoke his line without taking his eyes off Emmi.

I gave the Nurse's answer mechanically, watching the way Emmi and Flynn held each other in their gaze.

A moment later and everyone apart from Emmi and I had left the stage.

As Emmi gave her next few lines, asking about Romeo – wanting to know his name and if he was married – she turned to me at last. Her face was flushed, her voice risen with excitement.

A few moments later and we were done. As I followed Emmi to the edge of the stage, I searched for Flynn, but all I could see was the scenery for the balcony scene which was coming up in a moment. The stage manager, Maz, had created a balcony out of some painted cardboard and a set of steps on wheels. Right now he was trying to push his construction onto the stage. Liam, the boy who ran the props cupboard and was, supposedly, Maz's assistant, was preventing him.

'We don't need the balcony yet,' Liam hissed, pushing the scenery back into the wings so that it blocked the route off the stage.

Emmi and I stopped, unable to get any further.

'Yes we *do*,' Maz insisted. 'It should be on stage *now*.'

Beyond the painted cardboard I could see Flynn backstage, checking something in his script, clearly oblivious to the argument over the scenery.

Then, out of nowhere, Alex marched over and planted himself in front of Flynn. He said something I couldn't hear, but from the expression on his face he wasn't happy. I caught my breath as Flynn looked up slowly.

'Oh God,' Emmi murmured beside me.

'Act 2 scenery, come on!' Mr Nichols shouted from the hall.

'See?' Maz said triumphantly.

'We have to get past,' I insisted.

'Fine.' Liam released the scenery and Maz started manoeuvring it carefully round.

'Hurry up,' I hissed, my eyes on Flynn. He was trying to step past Alex, but Alex moved sideways, blocking Flynn's path. The two boys glared at each other. My pulse quickened. I knew that thundery look on Flynn's face. He was on the verge of exploding.

With a thud, the balcony scenery was out of our way. As Maz trundled it onto the stage, I scuttled past, only focused on getting to Flynn. There was a small crowd around him and Alex now. I was dimly aware of Emmi, beside me. Alex leaned closer to Flynn, speaking into his ear.

He looked furious.

I scurried towards them, pushing past people, determined to reach them before this went any further.

Too late. Flynn curled his lip and shoved out with both fists. They rammed into Alex's chest. Alex went flying into the crowd behind him. Flynn followed, fist clenched, arm raised, ready to punch.

'Hey!' Emmi's voice rose above the others – all clamouring indignantly.

'Quiet backstage!' Mr Nicols roared. 'And where

is Chorus? Come on, people! This is the *dress* run! We have to keep going!'

I elbowed my way through the throng. 'Flynn!'

He looked up at the sound of my voice, then turned back to Alex, who was scrambling upright, his own fists now curled into tight balls.

Flynn swung back his arm, making a fist, ready to punch. In a second the consequences of him hitting Alex in school flashed before my eyes: he'd be excluded . . . from the play . . . from school . . .

And he'd be ostracised even more than he was already. No one would understand. Alex was far more popular than Flynn.

I caught his wrist, just as Emmi reached Alex. I could dimly see her whispering rapidly in Alex's ear, but my focus was on Flynn. He stopped for a second, shocked, as I held his arm. Then he shook himself free.

With a final scornful glance at Alex, now virtually hidden from view by Emmi and a bunch of other people who'd swarmed between the two boys, Flynn turned and stormed off.

I scurried after him as the boy playing Chorus darted past me, all breathless, heading for the stage.

'Where are you going?' I said as Flynn burst through the door behind the stage and out of the hall. 'You're on again in a minute.'

215

He ignored me. I followed him, blinking in the sudden glare of the electric lights of the main school. The door slammed noisily behind us.

'Flynn?' I said. 'What just happened with Alex?' My pulse raced. Why was Alex so angry? What had Flynn done to upset him – was it something to do with Emmi?

Flynn shook his head and paced off along the school corridor. I stood for a second, frozen to the spot. Then I raced after him, the blood thundering in my ears.

'Flynn?' I hissed. 'Why won't you speak to me?'

Flynn stopped in mid-stride. He spun round, towering over me. Even in the heat of that moment I had time to register just how gorgeous he looked in his Romeo suit.

'I'm not in the mood for another fight,' he spat. 'This isn't about you, River . . . this is between me and Alex . . .'

A couple of boys I didn't recognise scuttled past us, open-mouthed. I forced myself to lower my voice.

'What did Alex say to you?'

'He said he didn't like me kissing Emmi in the play.' Flynn shook his head. 'Frigging prat.'

I stared at him. 'Why does that make him a prat? Of course he didn't like it.'

'You're taking *his* side?' Flynn's eyes widened with fury.

'No.' I shook my head vehemently. 'I'm just saying I understand. *I* didn't like you and her kissing either. There's no reason to get so angry about it.'

Flynn made a growling noise somewhere deep in his throat. His furious expression intensified. He slammed his hand against the wall. I jumped, my pulse racing.

'You're being stupid,' Flynn snarled. 'It's just a play.'

I stood for a moment, my heart pounding. I was frightened, I realised. Not that he would hit me, but that I couldn't be sure *what* he was going to do or say next.

'I'm *not* being stupid,' I said, my voice sharp as ice. 'In fact, I've just realised something.'

'And what's that?' Flynn growled.

'You're just like you describe your dad,' I said, the insight deepening as I spoke it. 'I mean, maybe you wouldn't actually hit me like he hit your mum, but you get out of control just like him . . . and . . . and you scare people.'

Flynn stared at me, his eyes hard and angry.

'Scare people?' he said.

'Scare *me*,' I admitted. 'Because you fly off the handle at the least little thing. Because you're so angry all the time.'

217

Flynn shook his head. 'That's ridiculous.'

There was a long pause, then the cloud lifted from his face. He pulled me towards him with a smile. 'Hey, after the dress run can we get out of here . . . go somewhere alone?'

I stared at him. How could he change just like that – from rage to seduction – in seconds.

Flynn raised his eyebrows. It was as if I hadn't challenged him. As if he hadn't been listening to me at all.

My heart sank as it hit me for the first time: maybe Flynn would never let me in and make me feel loved.

Maybe I was as close to him now as I was ever going to get.

22

I opened my mouth to try and explain what I was feeling. But before I could say anything one of the boys assisting the stage manager appeared. He cleared his throat nervously.

'Er, Flynn?' he stammered. 'Mr Nichols is looking for you . . . you were supposed to be on stage for Act 2 five minutes ago . . . er, we're meant to keep going . . . er, it's the dress rehearsal.'

'I know what it is,' Flynn snapped.

He leaned forward and kissed my cheek, then pushed past the boy and headed back to the hall. I waited a second, a jumble of feelings crowding my head. Then I crept back to the hall myself. I could hear Flynn in the distance, already on stage, performing.

'*Can I go forward when my heart is here?*' He sounded eager and excited – not a trace of the huge emotions of the moment just past in his voice.

I leaned against the props cupboard as Flynn disappeared across the stage. He'd be back in view in a minute, for the balcony scene in which Romeo and Juliet declare their love for each other.

I sank to the ground and put my head in my hands.

'River?'

I looked up. Grace was sidling up to me.

'Is it hard, seeing him with someone else?' she whispered sympathetically.

I turned away, trying to hide the fact that my eyes were filling with tears.

Grace patted my arm. 'Have you got a moment before you're on again?' she said. 'There's something I want to tell you. In private.'

I hesitated. I had to be back soon, as Nurse, to call Juliet from the side of the stage. On the other hand, I didn't think I could bear to watch the very next, highly romantic, exchange between Flynn and Emmi.

On an impulse, I jumped up and asked Daisy Walker to say my lines for me.

'It's just a couple of words from off-stage, Daisy,' I pleaded. 'No one will notice and I really need to talk to Grace about something.'

Daisy gave me a searching look, but agreed without asking any questions.

Relieved, I followed Grace out of the hall. As we walked along the corridor, it struck me that I was going to have to watch Emmi and Flynn together many times over the next few nights. There would be at least five more kisses tonight and then two performances full of them. I couldn't bear it.

'What is it?' I asked Grace, trying not to think about the kisses.

'Not here.' Grace led me down to the girls' dressing room – a tiny classroom near the assembly hall. The windows had been covered with black felt to give us privacy. Although it was still light outside, the room itself was shadowy and still.

Grace shifted a box containing Emmi's spare make-up off a chair and sat me down. She took the chair opposite, then leaned forward excitedly.

I stared at her, my own worries receding momentarily as I noticed her flushed cheeks and eager eyes.

'What's up, Grace?' I said.

'James and I did it last night,' she said.

I looked at her. Her pale face was glowing. *God*. She looked . . . well . . . radiant.

'You mean for the first time?' I said awkwardly, feeling I should know. I'd been so preoccupied with Flynn for the past few weeks that I hadn't been aware of anything Grace was doing.

Grace nodded. 'The first time with *anyone*.'

'Wow,' I said. 'How was it?'

'Amazing,' Grace breathed. Then she screwed up her face. 'Messy, though.'

I grinned at her. 'So are you in love?'

Grace rolled her eyes. 'Oh, I don't know. But he's sweet. And kind. And gentle. Oh Riv, last night. I can't tell you. He was just so . . . so . . .'

'Grateful?' I suggested.

'No.' Grace drew back, looking scandalised. 'Well, yes. But it was more than that. He was so . . . so loving. He made me feel so special. Not in some bigshot I'd-die-for-you way. But just small things, like how he kept asking if I was okay, even when we were . . . you know, right in the middle of it . . . and how he made me feel we could wait if I wanted and I could trust him completely – you know, that he'd never look at anyone else and . . .'

I bit my lip, trying to push down the tears that were welling up. Why wasn't Flynn like that? He was all about the bigshot I'd-die-for-you gestures. But I was beginning to see that a lot of his passion came from anger. Where were the small kindnesses? Why wasn't he saying that he'd wait for sex until I was ready? Why didn't I trust him with Emmi? Why hadn't he told me he loved me?

'River, what is it?' Grace was bending forward, her blonde hair swishing against my mud-brown.

222

'Nothing,' I said, biting harder on my lip, trying not to cry. 'Listen, I'm really pleased about you and James. He's a sweet guy.'

Grace made a small face. 'He is, but . . .' She hesitated. 'What about Flynn? I mean, he's not sweet maybe, but he's really into you too, isn't he?'

A tear trickled down my face. I couldn't hold it in any longer.

'I love him so much, Grace,' I sobbed. 'I love him so much.'

Grace's expression softened. 'But doesn't he love you?' she frowned. 'I thought you two were okay.'

I told her. Not about Flynn's family and his past – but how he'd got angry earlier and how, even though he'd opened up to me recently, he seemed to think I should give him sex in return. It was funny. As I said the words, I realised they were true. He did see it as some kind of bargain, I was sure. That was why he'd started mentioning sex almost as soon as he'd told me about his dad.

Grace frowned. 'But I'm sure he's crazy about you, Riv. Anyone can see it. Maybe he just doesn't know how to say he loves you.'

I shook my head. Flynn always knew what to say. He was good with words.

'Come on, Riv,' Grace insisted. 'James says Flynn's never been like this about anyone.'

'Does he?' I looked up. 'What's Flynn said to him?'

Grace coloured a little. 'Well, it's not so much that Flynn's *said* anything . . .'

'You see?' I started sobbing again. 'He hasn't said he loves me. Not to me. Not to anyone. Because he doesn't. He just wants sex. I bet he'd do it with anyone.' I gripped Grace's arm. 'Swear you'll tell me the truth, if I ask you something?'

'What?' Grace's eyes widened.

'Swear?'

'Okay.' She shrugged. 'I swear. What d'you . . .?'

'Does Emmi fancy him?' I blurted out.

Grace's snubby nose wrinkled with distaste. 'River. She'd never . . .'

'Yeah. But does she fancy him?' I said. 'Cos if she does, he'll know when they kiss on stage. I *know* he will. And . . . God . . . if *he* wants *her* . . .' My breath was coming in great heavy gasps now. 'Oh God, if he wants her . . .'

'Hey, River. Riv . . .' Grace pulled me into a hug. 'It's not worth all this, babe. No guy is.'

I slid onto the floor, weeping my guts out. 'He is, Grace. Oh God, I love him so much. So much.'

I was practically hysterical. It was like all the tension of the last two months was flooding out of me – all the exhausting attempts not to mention the things that made Flynn angry and all the worry about how he felt and what he wanted.

Then the door opened and Emmi walked in.

She took one look at me in a heap on the floor and staggered dramatically back against the door.

'Ohmigod, he's dumped you.'

'Shut up, Emmi,' Grace said, with surprising firmness.

She got up and stalked over to Emmi. I could hear them whispering together. I was still crying on the floor. I didn't even know why I was crying any more. Just that I'd wanted to love someone and be loved back. I'd wanted that so much. And I'd thought it was happening with Flynn. I really did. And now it was like all my feelings were out there, raw, and I was still totally alone.

Yes, I'd turned my soul inside out because of him. And yet somehow it wasn't enough. I couldn't be sure he loved me.

Emmi swished over, her silky Juliet dress gleaming in the light that bled around the black felt curtains. She squatted down beside me.

'Riv?'

I looked up into her large, chocolatey eyes. She was frowning, but she still looked pretty – her sleek brown hair all soft and curling round her pointy little face. How could Flynn not fancy her?

'I'm sure he loves you,' she said. 'Just as I'm certain he's not interested in me. Alex says he's never been like this about anyone.'

'And how would Alex know?' I said angrily. 'It's not like they're best friends. Look what just happened backstage – they were practically fighting because Alex was jealous.'

Emmi sighed. 'It wasn't so much he was jealous . . .' She twisted her hair in her hand. 'I mean, I know Alex isn't exactly Mr Emotional Intelligence . . . on the other hand, there are some things he does incredibly well.'

I rolled my eyes. 'Please, Emmi, I don't want to hear about your sex life again.'

'I don't mean that,' she said. 'I mean that Alex is straightforward and uncomplicated. I like that. No hidden depths. No sudden surprises. He just wanted to make sure Flynn knew he was, like, top dog or something . . . And . . . okay, so maybe he can be a bit heavy, but at least he doesn't fly off the handle at the tiniest little thing.'

I stared at her, my eyes narrowing. 'You mean like Flynn does.'

Emmi shrugged. 'You gotta admit Flynn's a weird guy, River. He's not like other people. That not-drinking thing. Plus, he's intense. He's moody. He can be really rude and arrogant . . .'

'He's passionate,' I spat, suddenly incensed. 'And he's loyal. He works so hard in ways you can't even imagine and he feels things so deeply and . . .' I stopped, confused by the grin that had spread across Emmi's face. 'What?'

'If he isn't madly in love with you, he should be,' Emmi said. 'D'you know how alike you two are?'

I frowned. I'd always thought of Flynn as being like Emmi – clever and quick and charming.

'Seriously.' Emmi laughed. 'If you could see your face. All red and angry and defending him. By the way, you must be due back on stage pretty soon, you'd better fix your . . .'

'*No*.' I was already up in the chair, my hands reaching for the big block of make-up.

'Oh my God,' I said, staring into the mirror. 'Look at the state of me.' My eyes were all puffy and my cheeks streaked with tear stains.

Emmi and Grace both stood behind me. They exchanged knowing looks. Then Emmi folded her arms.

'What exactly is it that you want, River?'

I slapped on some foundation. 'I want to know he loves me,' I said steadily. 'I want to know that he really, truly, deeply loves me.'

'Why don't you ask him?' Grace said.

I caught Emmi's eye.

'Because he'll just tell me what he thinks I want to hear. And I need proof.'

Grace wrinkled her nose. 'But how can you get proof that someone loves you?'

I smoothed out the make-up over my face and picked up some eyeshadow. Then I looked up at Emmi's reflection in the mirror. I could tell she knew what I was thinking.

I raised my eyebrows at her, asking the question. *Will you do it?*

'I don't fancy him, River,' she said slowly. 'And even if I did, I would never, ever . . .'

'I know,' I said to her reflection. 'I believe you.' And I did. It was clear to me now – Emmi had never been interested in Flynn.

But that didn't mean he wasn't interested in her.

'I know you wouldn't go after Flynn,' I said again, fixing Emmi with my gaze. 'That's why it'll work.'

23

The first night of the play was a big success. I was so nervous I was nearly sick, but once I was on stage, actually speaking my lines, I started to relax and enjoy it.

Flynn and Emmi were both brilliant, and everyone did better than in the rehearsals. Even James managed to make himself heard halfway down the hall.

'Doing it with you obviously gives him confidence,' I whispered to Grace as we watched Act 3, Scene 1 from the wings.

James as Mercutio and Alex as Tybalt drew their swords. Flynn was on stage too. I was only a metre or so away, backstage, but he had no idea I was standing there – all his focus was on his friends. On his lines.

I watched him turning from one to the other, desperate to stop their fight.

'*Gentlemen, for shame, forbear this outrage!*'

The language was so old-fashioned – so ludicrous really – coming out of Flynn's mouth. And yet he somehow managed to make it sound like what it meant: 'Stop it, guys. You're out of order.'

Alex stabbed James and rushed off to the other side of the stage, where Emmi was standing, her lips moving as she went over her long speech that started the next scene.

Then James staggered offstage – into Grace's arms, in fact. She was already there, standing with me and waiting for her next cue.

Flynn faced the audience alone. Guilty. Desperate. Angry. In love. Each emotion was there, flowing in and out of his face and his voice. He was totally commanding. Utterly convincing. I'd never seen him act this well.

I looked across the stage to the wings, opposite. Emmi was watching Flynn too. Our eyes met. Up until that moment I hadn't really thought I'd go through with our plan. But seeing Flynn's performance here – as subtle and intense as his face – I knew that I had to do it. That I would never be sure of him, otherwise. He was just too good an actor for me to trust anything he said.

Emmi raised her eyes. 'Tonight?' she mouthed.

I shook my head. Mum and Dad were watching

tonight – and would expect me to go home with them afterwards.

'Friday,' I mouthed back.

We talked through the details later, during the start of Act 5, when Flynn was on stage and we weren't.

James Molloy was having a party after Friday night's final performance. Grace knew his house and said there was a perfect place for us to carry out the plan – two adjoining office areas, all quiet and secluded.

The plan itself was simple. Emmi was going to make out that she fancied Flynn, while I watched. If he tried to get off with her, I would know that being with me was just about sex. If he said no, I would know I'd been worrying about nothing.

I would know that he loved me.

The second night was as big a success as the first. Both audiences were full and appreciative – well, it was a big school and I guess parents always like watching their kids perform.

I hated it, though. I watched Flynn and Emmi kiss seven times – jealousy twisting in my heart – and each time I counted it off on my fingers. Emmi had sworn that there was nothing in the kisses. Soon I would know for sure.

Mr Nichols got tipsy on champagne in the second half and hugged me and Emmi as we trooped offstage after our curtain call.

'You were brilliant,' he rasped – his voice still hadn't come back completely after all the shouting last week.

Emmi went off to get changed and Mr Nichols offered me a rueful smile.

'Don't tell anyone, but I'm sorry I didn't make you Juliet,' he whispered. 'She was good, but you'd have been better.'

I shrugged, not knowing what to say. What did it matter now, anyway?

I saw Flynn's mum briefly after the show.

'Now we can't stop long, River. I had to swap my shift so I'm at work later, but wasn't he grand? And weren't you? You made me laugh with your huffing and puffing and forgetting and with poor Juliet desperate for news of your man.'

She wanted to speak to Mr Nichols too, but Flynn hustled her away before she had a chance, stopping on his way to the exit only to extricate Siobhan from where she was standing, tongue-tied, in front of a small knot of admiring St Cletus's sixth-formers.

He got them outside, then darted back in to say goodbye to me.

His face was flushed and shining from where he had scrubbed off his stage make-up in a hurry.

'I'll be back later,' he breathed, dragging me into a corner. 'I'm going off my head not seeing you.'

I hugged him, feeling guilty that I was planning to trick him. Maybe it was mean of me. Maybe I should just ask him how he felt, like Grace had suggested.

Flynn glanced over his shoulder. The hall was full of people milling about. No one was watching us. He pressed me back against the wall and kissed my neck. 'Come back to mine, later, after the party,' he whispered. 'Yeah? Mum'll be working a night shift and Caitlin and Siob are both staying over at friends'. I've sorted it.' He pressed up against me and gave this little groan. 'It'll be after the play, then, like you said. Yeah, River? Yeah?'

I could hear the lust catching at his throat. My guilt vanished. He was totally setting me up. All he was thinking about was having sex. He didn't care about me. Whether it was really what I wanted. How I felt.

'Sure.' I forced a smile and pushed him away. 'I'll tell Mum I'm staying over at Emmi's.'

James Molloy's party was fantastic. His parents had gone away for the weekend, leaving him and his brothers alone in this big detached house on the edge of town. Loads of people came. The whole of the cast, plus most of the people who'd helped backstage and lots of St Cletus sixth-formers. There were plenty of other girls too – some from our school, and others I didn't recognise.

Everyone was on a high. Music was pounding out, a fast bass vibrating under my feet – and there was loads to drink. Emmi was under strict instructions not to get off her face – I knew Flynn wouldn't even speak to her if she was. She grumbled a bit, but agreed to keep to orange juice.

'Only for half an hour, though,' she said, glaring at me. 'So you better get him into that room.'

I nodded, then caught sight of Flynn watching me from across the room. He walked towards me, his eyes not flickering away for a second. My stomach flipped over – *God*, I wanted him so badly. For a few moments I completely forgot how cross I was about him setting me up for our first time tonight. How insecure I was about how he felt about me. All I could think about was him getting here and kissing and touching me. But when he drew up beside me he did neither. Instead, he leaned against the wall and took a gulp of his Coke.

'Are you glad it's over?' he said.

'The play?' I shrugged. I didn't know how I felt about it. The truth was it didn't feel over. Not yet.

I looked around the living room where we were standing. It was big – with three gigantic squishy sofas and a long, shiny wooden sideboard.

'You had a nerve giving me all that rubbish about my house,' I said lightly. 'James's place is twice the size.'

Flynn grinned and drank some more, looking around at the people dancing and the couples already sprawled all over the sofas.

'Believe me,' he said, 'I was far harder on James. Anyway . . .' he raised his eyebrows, '. . . are you ready to leave yet?'

I mock-glared at him. 'We only just got here.' I hesitated. 'Still, okay . . . I left my bag in that little office room near the kitchen. Maybe, when we've finished our drinks, you could get it? Then we could go?'

Flynn raised his plastic cup and drained it.

'See you in a minute.'

He loped off. I watched him cross the room. It took some time. People kept stopping him, congratulating him on his performance. Several girls touched his arm as he spoke to them.

At last he was at the door. He disappeared.

I darted over to Emmi. She was wrapped round Alex like a snake.

'Emmi,' I hissed.

She disentangled herself and leaned over.

'It's time,' I whispered.

She turned back to Alex and made some excuse, then we sped out of the living room.

We passed the first office. Through the half-open door I could just make out Flynn's back. He was bent over, rummaging among a pile of coats for my bag. Which wasn't, of course, actually there.

Emmi gripped my hand. 'Are you sure, Riv?' she whispered.

I nodded, then went next door, into the second, smaller office. I locked the door behind me, then crept over to the door between the two rooms. Grace had already been in there and left it open. It was just slightly ajar – giving enough space for me to peer through. The study I was in was dark. The one where Flynn was still searching for my bag was brightly lit.

He was looking under the desk now, pulling out a heap of rucksacks, swearing under his breath.

Emmi appeared in the other doorway.

'Hey, Romeo,' she drawled. 'I was looking for you.'

24

Flynn spun round and stood up. He ran his hand self-consciously through his hair. 'Hi,' he said. 'Have you seen River's bag?'

Emmi closed the door behind her.

My mouth fell open as she sashayed towards him. I hadn't really clocked what she was wearing before. She was in a pair of those spiky heels she'd bought a few weeks ago – her hips swinging in this short, flirty little dress. Her hair looked stunning. Her lips were all soft and pouty.

How was he going to resist her?

My stomach screwed up into a knot. Flynn was staring at her. They were both sideways on to me. I could see Flynn reading her face, looking bewildered. And Emmi, her eyes hard, slinking right up in front of him.

'What are you doing, Emmi?' Flynn said uncertainly.

Emmi put her hand on his arm. She flicked back her hair. 'I was looking for you,' she said throatily. She glanced back at the shut door behind her. 'I wanted to see you on your own.'

I held my breath. Emmi was acting, I knew. But she was doing it far, far better than anything I'd seen her do on stage as Juliet. There was no way Flynn wouldn't believe she was genuinely throwing herself at him. No way he could be unaware that all he had to do was lean forward and . . .'

I clutched at the door frame that stood between us.

Flynn frowned. 'Why d'you want to see me? What's going on?'

Emmi sighed. She ran her hand up his arm, then rested her fingers round his neck. 'Did you like kissing me?' she said softly. 'In the play?'

I gripped the door frame more tightly. My knuckles shone white in the light coming from the next room. If Flynn had looked round, he would have seen my fingertips round the edge of the door. But he didn't look round.

He was only looking at Emmi.

'I thought you were River's friend,' he said.

Emmi shrugged. 'River won't know.' She looked up at him slyly. Then she put her other hand round his waist. 'No one will know.'

238

I could see Flynn blinking. His face all confused and wary.

It was going to happen in the next few seconds. Either he would pull away. Or he would lean forwards and . . .'

What the hell was I doing?

I burst through the door. 'Hi,' I said.

Flynn jumped about a mile in the air. Emmi spun round.

'River?' she hissed.

'Get out,' I said.

Emmi spread her hands in a gesture of absolute exasperation.

'I'm sorry,' I said to her. 'I shouldn't have . . . I'm sorry.'

She rolled her eyes at me, then turned and walked out of the room without a word.

I stared down at the carpet. Flynn was just half a metre in front of me. I couldn't look at him. My whole face was burning with shame.

'River?' He put his hands on my arms. I stared down at the carpet. A corner of the desk stood to my right, a jumble of rucksacks beneath it. On my left was the bottom shelf of a bookcase.

In front of me were Flynn's feet. His cheap trainers.

'I'm sorry,' I whispered.

I felt his hands fall from my arms. His feet took a step backwards.

'What *was* all that?' he said. 'Why were you saying sorry to Emmi?'

I looked up at him. His face registered shock. Confusion. And then his eyes hardened.

'You knew what Emmi was doing, didn't you?' His face was like thunder. 'Why?'

I couldn't speak. My heart was choking my throat.

'Were you laughing at me?' It was hardly more than a whisper. 'Were you playing some game?'

'No.' I found my voice suddenly. 'It was a test. I wanted to see if you'd go with Emmi. I . . . I . . . it was stupid. Okay?'

Flynn took another step away from me. 'A test?' he said hoarsely. 'A test of what?'

'To see if you loved me,' I said. My voice was shaking. My whole body was shaking. 'Look. It was stupid. It was wrong. I stopped her before . . .'

'You're frigging right it was wrong,' Flynn shouted. 'I can't believe you would . . . that you would *test* me. That you would get Emmi to . . . to . . . God, River. What is your *problem*?'

I couldn't look at him. I suddenly saw how I must seem to him – jealous and insecure and stupid.

'And what does it prove, anyway?' he yelled. 'Me turning Emmi down – which I would have

240

done – only proves I don't fancy her. At least not enough to risk losing you over. How does that tell you I love you?'

I shook my head. I could feel his eyes boring into me. My heart seemed to shrink away to dust. I'd blown it. I'd thrown it away.

Flynn's voice dropped to a whisper. 'How could you not know that I love you? It's there every time I look at you. Every time we touch each other. From the first moment I saw you.' Flynn shook his head. 'How could you not feel it?'

He stared at me for a long moment then his whole face closed up.

He strode over to the door.

'Wait.' I ran after him. 'Please, Flynn,' I sobbed. 'I *did* feel it, sometimes, but you never *said*. Don't you see? I mean, *Emmi* was Juliet. And any guy who turned down Emmi would have to be mad, or so into someone else that . . .'

'How would you feel if I'd done that to you?' Flynn's eyes flashed angrily. He put his hand on the doorknob. 'How would you feel if I'd got some guy to try it on with you, just to see what you did?'

'I know,' I wept, tears leaking down my face. 'I just wanted to . . . to be sure of how you felt.'

'Jesus Christ, River.' Flynn exploded. 'Can you hear the total rubbish you're coming out with? You can *never* be sure of someone else. *Never.* You have to have trust . . . faith . . . That's what love is about. It's a frigging leap in the dark.'

He turned the door handle.

'You make it sound like a religion,' I said quickly.

Flynn turned to face me. 'At least religion has heat and fire and passion. The worst thing about this – about you setting me up with Emmi – is that it's so cold-blooded.'

'It's no more cold-blooded than you trying to have sex with me,' I muttered.

Flynn's eyes widened. 'What?'

I stared up at him sullenly. 'You got it all planned, didn't you? Get everyone out of the house. Get a shag. Get happy. Great. Except what about me? What about what I want?'

Flynn blinked. 'I thought that *was* what you wanted. I thought . . .'

We stared at each other. Flynn's forehead creased with a frown.

'You didn't listen,' I said, my insides twisting horribly. 'I told you . . . I tried to tell you . . . I wasn't ready.'

Flynn's frown deepened. 'But . . . but you said after the play . . .'

'I didn't mean *right* after,' I said. 'I meant . . .'

But I couldn't say what I meant. Suddenly I didn't

know what I meant. 'It's not that I don't want to,' I said, trying desperately to explain. 'It's just that . . . sometimes I think for you it's only about sex. Like as soon as you told me about your dad, as soon as you'd opened up, you acted as if . . . as if I should automatically be ready to go the whole way . . . and I'm just . . . I'm not ready . . . not yet . . .'

Flynn sighed. 'Well, why didn't you *say* that? Why didn't you just say: *no, Flynn, you horny git, I'm not ready?*'

'Because I was scared you'd go off me,' I whispered. 'You're so . . . you're so moody . . . and angry . . . all the time.' I slid my arms round his back, then reached up inside his shirt, feeling for the scar on his shoulder.

Juliet's lines echoed in my head:

My bounty is as boundless as the sea
My love as deep; the more I give to thee
The more I have, for both are infinite.

I traced the line of his scar.

He stood, all stiff and awkward, but he didn't push me away.

A long moment passed.

'I know I'm angry . . .' he mumbled. 'It's . . . you were right . . . I mean, what you said before about me flaring up and being scary . . . like my dad . . . I know that's true . . .'

243

I looked up at him. 'You said what I said was stupid.'

Flynn made a face. 'Yeah, well, I don't like it . . . how you see into me . . . it freaks me out . . .'

'But understanding each other is a good thing, isn't it?'

Flynn said nothing, just hugged me tighter.

'So . . .' I hesitated. 'So . . . why do you get so angry?'

'I dunno . . .' Flynn's voice was low and miserable. 'I dunno . . . it's just always there . . .'

I leaned against his chest. 'I thought when I loved somebody it would be perfect,' I whispered. 'Like it is in . . . in the play. I thought it would be easy. We'd just know what to do. And we'd agree about every-thing. And—'

Flynn snorted. 'You're a frigging nutjob, River. You know that? A nutjob.'

He wound his arms round my neck.

We stood in silence for a while.

The music thumped away in the background. I could hear people laughing and shouting in the corridor outside.

Then Flynn sighed. 'So . . . on top of thinking that I'm moody and rude and difficult – you also think I'm capable of doing it with your best friend behind your back and dumping you because you're not

244

quite ready to have sex with me.' He looked down at me and grinned. 'Have I left anything out?'

A trickle of relief seeped slowly through my brain as I looked up into his eyes. 'Did I mention I think you're hopelessly screwed up?' I said.

Flynn leaned down and kissed my neck.

'Oh, I think we've established that we're both frigging screwed up,' he murmured.

I twisted my head, searching for his mouth.

We kissed for a long time.

Finally Flynn drew back. 'You could still come back to my place.' He smiled at me, hopefully. 'No pressure, but we could just sleep together. You know, all curled up.'

I grinned. Back in September I'd imagined love as one feeling. One big, grand, uncomplicated feeling. But it wasn't like that at all. It's made up of lots of feelings: trust and sex and fun and regret and forgiving and hope and . . . well, pretty much everything, really.

And, if you're with the right person, it's somehow bigger than all those things put together, too.

'I guess we'd better say goodbye to everyone else, then,' I said. 'My bag's in the kitchen. No. Honest, Flynn. It is. Under the sink.'

Flynn opened the door and slipped away to get my bag. I blinked into the dim light of the hall.

Music seemed to be blaring out from all directions. Then I caught sight of Emmi and Grace, huddled together on the stairs. They saw me and came running over.

Emmi shook my arm. 'Why d'you stop me, Riv?' she pouted. 'It was looking good. I mean, I could see he thought I was hot, but I'm pretty sure there was no way he'd have . . .'

'I know.' I laughed. 'I just realised it was the wrong thing to do.'

Grace and Emmi exchanged glances. I grinned, suddenly feeling ridiculously happy. After all my worries I knew that Flynn loved me. And that I had two good friends who really cared about me.

I threw my arms around them both and hugged them tightly. 'Thanks, guys,' I beamed.

They drew back suspiciously.

'So you're okay about how he feels about you?' Grace said tentatively.

I nodded.

'And you've stopped worrying that he likes me because I was Juliet?' Emmi asked.

I nodded.

'And you don't mind that he wants to . . . you know . . .' Grace blushed.

'. . . shag you senseless,' Emmi added.

I shook my head.

Emmi pursed her lips. 'I still think he's trouble,' she said.

'So angry,' Grace nodded. 'And moody. And intense.'

'Like the night,' Emmi said darkly. She started quoting melodramatically from *Romeo and Juliet*.

'Come, gentle night, come, loving black-brow'd night,
Give me my Romeo.'

I grinned at her, remembering the next lines:
And, when he shall die,
Take him and cut him out in little stars
And he will make the face of heaven so fine
That all the world will be in love with night . . .

Then I caught sight of Flynn by the front door.

And I forgot the play and the poetry.

And all I wanted was another kiss.

Award-winning books from Sophie McKenzie

GIRL, MISSING

Winner Richard and Judy Best Kids' Books 2007 12+
Winner of the Red House Children's Book Award 2007 12+
Winner of the Manchester Children's Book Award 2008
Winner of the Bolton Children's Book Award
Winner of the Grampian Children's Book Award 2008
Winner of the John Lewis Solihull Book Award 2008
Winner of the Lewisham Children's Book Award
Winner of the 2008 Sakura Medal

SIX STEPS TO A GIRL

Winner of the Manchester Children's Book Award 2009

BLOOD TIES

Overall winner of the Red House Children's Book Award 2009
Winner of the Leeds Book Award 2009 age 11–14 category
Winner of the Spellbinding Award 2009
Winner of the Lancashire Children's Book Award 2009
Winner of the Portsmouth Book Award 2009 (Longer Novel section)
Winner of the Staffordshire Children's Book Award 2009
Winner of the Southern Schools Book Award 2010
Winner of the RED Book Award 2010
Winner of the Warwickshire Secondary Book Award 2010
Winner of the Grampian Children's Book Award 2010
Winner of the North East Teenage Book Award 2010

THE MEDUSA PROJECT: THE SET-UP

Winner of the North-East Book Award 2010
Winner of the Portsmouth Book Award 2010

ABOUT THE AUTHOR

Sophie McKenzie was born and brought up in London, where she still lives with her teenage son. She has worked as a journalist and a magazine editor, but fell in love with writing after being made redundant and enrolling on a creative writing course, and now writes thriller and relationship novels for young adults. She burst into the publishing world with *Girl, Missing* (published 2006), which tallied up numerous award wins nationwide and was longlisted for the coveted Carnegie Medal. The sequel, *Sister, Missing*, was published in hardcover in Autumn 2011. *Blood Ties* (2008) was another multiple award-winner which again saw Sophie longlisted for the Carnegie Medal, and crowned winner of the North East Teen Book Award and the Red House Book Award amongst many others. Its follow-up, *Blood Ransom*, was published in 2010. *Falling Fast* is the first title in her new Flynn series.